On the Terror Trail

ON THE TERROR TRAIL

Tracy Dunham

AVALON BOOKS
THOMAS BOUREGY AND COMPANY, INC.
401 LAFAYETTE STREET
NEW YORK, NEW YORK 10003

© Copyright 1989 by Tracy Dunham
Library of Congress Catalog Card Number: 89-85874
ISBN 0-8034-8784-3
All rights reserved.
All the characters in this book are fictitious,
and any resemblance to actual persons,
living or dead, is purely coincidental.

PRINTED IN THE UNITED STATES OF AMERICA
BY HADDON CRAFTSMEN, SCRANTON, PENNSYLVANIA

For Paul

Chapter One

THE straw in the barn was musty and hot, but Leland Moses settled down for the night. His horse whickered softly to him in the dark, as though reassuring his master he was welcome to share his bed. Tipping his hat over his eyes, Moses tried to sleep. It was loneliest at moments like this, when he was in a small town.

As he often did, he remembered how he got here, to another tiny bit of civilization in the Oklahoma Territory, hunting a wanted man. It had been only a couple of years before that he had decided not to reenlist in the Tenth Cavalry, the only job he'd ever known as a free man. He saw the scene over and over as he tried to sleep.

Sergeant Leland Moses of the Tenth Cavalry was tilted back on his camp chair. The summer raids were over, the winter campaign not yet ordered, and he knew it was time. Well nigh time, he thought, pulling his hat more firmly onto his head. It was getting too cozy. *Men like me, we can't be at ease for too long, can't feel like we belong, because we don't and never will.* When he was supposed to re-up, he'd wire his old captain from the Great War. Captain Wilmuth had told him any time he wanted to be a Federal Marshal, he'd make sure he got the position. Money was the only way he'd ever get what he really wanted, a piece of land to call his own, and he'd never have that, chasing Indians all over territory whites were settling, carving out their pieces of God's country.

Colonel Grierson had done his best to talk him out of it. Offered him his choice of the newest crop of three-year-olds, told him he was the best danged sergeant in the United States Army. But when Moses had made it clear that he was moving on, the old man had taken his hand in a firm shake. "You ever want back in, Sergeant Moses, you let me know. The Army can't lose too many men like you."

Saluting, he'd felt a pang of regret at his decision. But it was better to go it alone again; he knew it from the soles of his feet to his fingertips. Feeling comfortable, feeling right, didn't work for Leland Moses. He'd chase whatever kind of scum were on the Wanted posters and running from a United States Marshal. He would start investing in his own future, and not that of the United States Army.

The telegraph had been sent to Wilmuth. Once again, Leland Moses was hunting, as he had since his childhood. And once again, as it had been during the war, it was for men.

Mentally shelving his memories, Moses dug a

On the Terror Trail

hole for his shoulder in the straw of that barn in the Oklahoma Territory, and forced himself to try to sleep. His badge cut its sharp edges into his chest as he folded his arms. He had a few hours before the saloons were packed and his man would be most likely to show.

The night sounds of the livery failed to lull him to sleep. Somewhere, a dog's bark bit into the night. He'd have the bounty money for the cattle rustler wired to his bank in St. Louis. The account was growing slowly but steadily, and soon he'd have enough to buy a small place, some breeding stock, a home. It was a hard question as to whether his reputation would outstrip his bank balance first, however. Bounty hunting, even when wearing a badge, was a quick way to die, and he knew it. He'd wait until noon for the sheriff to receive the confirmatory telegram on the man he was about to take in, and then he'd head out once more, track down another wanted man. It wasn't too far to the next semblance of civilization; he was sure to find the next man.

Night hit hard on the small, one-street village in the Oklahoma Territory. A few small lights flickered gamely from the oilcloth windows of the shanties, casting grotesque reflections on the face of the cowpoke riding in for a late drink. Leland Moses watched from the blackness of the livery door, his hand cupped about the orange glow of his cigarette. The horses inside had heard the clipped trot of the dun ridden by the cowboy, and they gave gentle nickers of greeting from their stalls. Moses once more pulled the worn Wanted poster from his vest pocket, and studied the crudely drawn features of the outlaw.

He had him. Checking his revolver, the ex-sergeant felt his pulse quicken. It was always like this before he made his move, the wondering if the outlaw would draw, or be taken in peaceably. Not many wanted a black Federal Marshal to rope them to their horse and haul them back to stand trial for horse thieving or cattle rustling. More often than not, he ended up with a carcass and more money if there was a reward, saving the government the time and expense of trying the doomed man and buying the rope to hang him. But still, it wasn't his way. He liked to think he gave the man a chance to lay down his weapons and give it up.

The dank, smoke-filled air of the filthy saloon made him want to gag. Standing in the doorway, back to the dark street, Moses knew he was a ready target. But mostly the hombres weren't looking for a black Federal Marshal to be dogging their trails, so for a minute he was able to check out the other occupants of the Golden Rule Saloon. Playing poker in the corner, three cowboys drunkenly laid down their cards. A loner nursed a bottle of rye at one hand-hewn table, while two more rough types slugged down their drinks at the bar. Moses carefully scruti-

On the Terror Trail 5

nized the lone wolf, checking the separate parts of his face and description against the poster.

"Hey, you, not in my saloon, you don't!" The barkeep, a fat, balding Irishman, stepped quickly from behind the railing. "I'll not be serving my liquor to you!"

Moving quickly, Moses pulled his Colt and flashed the badge. "Federal Marshal." Nodding in the direction of the lone man, he added, "I've got a warrant for this man's arrest."

All movement had died with the appearance of the unholstered gun. Moses shifted his gaze from the outlaw to the Irishman, not willing to take the chance that the barkeep would stay out of it.

"That's the biggest bunch of blarney I've heard in years, laddie. Now get your tail out of here, afore I call in the sheriff."

"Mister, outta my way. Interfering with a Federal Marshal is against the law, and if you don't believe me, you'll die. My color doesn't mean a thing, not with this badge here. Now get out of my way!"

The outlaw's hands had dropped from the bottle to his lap. Sweat shone on his upper lip through the rough growth of beard.

Firing off a shot, Moses blew away the bottle of rye. "Get your hands on the table, Sorrell, or you're next." Whisky ran from the table and settled in dirty pools on the sawdust floor.

Screeching back in the chair, Sorrell started to rise, reaching for his gun.

"Stay put, Sorrell. Hands on the table, I said!" Seemingly oblivious to the others in the room, Moses' dark eyes burned into the scruffy-looking character, waiting for the moment of decision to cross the outlaw's face.

"I ain't about to take nothing off you!"

The outlaw had decided. Moses fired into the man's gut. The recoil of his twitching figure sent tables and chairs clattering. Crouching swiftly, the marshal aimed at the barkeep.

"Your turn next, Irish?" His deep, soft voice cut through the stale air like an English razor. Suddenly pale, the barkeep retreated behind the rough wood planks nailed to one side of the room. Watching his hands, Moses waited for the shotgun he knew was hidden.

"Don't try it, Irish—remember Sorrell here. Now just be a good fellow, and see if you can roust your sheriff out of bed, or whatever, and get him down here."

"Ain't you even gonna see if he's alive?" Righteous indignation filled every word of the blustery barkeep.

"No need. He's dead. Now get on down the street here, move it."

"I don't take orders from you." Folding his arms over the dirty apron, the barkeep ensconced himself more firmly behind the bar.

Moses considered the chances of forcing the

man to help him. It made no difference to him, as long as he didn't get backshot hauling the dead man into the sheriff's office for identification. Kicking aside the overturned tables, Moses grabbed a handful of the dead man's shirt from behind. As he dragged the dead weight across the slimy floor, Moses' eyes darted from man to man. It was always like this, the outlaw looking like the good guy, and he was the bad man because he was black. It would have made his job a lot easier if he'd been born white, but at least the Federals paid the same bounty, no matter what the color of the man bringing in the proof of death.

The dead cowboy's heels jerked and bumped down the street as Moses laboriously hauled his body to the sheriff. He'd need a witness to the identification of the man in order to collect, since he had no intention of hauling a corpse back to St. Louis. He already knew, however, what would happen once he awakened the sheriff.

Answering the door of the jail after a pounding that would have awakened the dead, the sheriff stood slack-jawed in wonder at the sight before him. A tall, large-boned black man stood there, his weapon pulled, dragging a dead white man behind him like a sack of flour.

"What's going on here, fella? What kind of mischief you gotten into, too much liquor? Well, just hold on there a minute, and I'll—"

"Leland Moses, United States Marshal. I'm

here with Lee Sorrell, wanted dead or alive. Need you to identify him, send a wire to St. Louis."

"I'll be danged. . . ." The sheriff stared in amazement at the educated words, the lack of deference in the black man's manner. "Say that again?"

"I'm Marshal Leland Moses. I've got a warrant here for this man, dead or alive. Now, please, fill out all your reports and get them wired into St. Louis, so this body doesn't have to stay above ground much longer."

The sheriff stared for the first time at the drifter, crumpled in a pool of blood on his wooden floor. "Sorrell, you say? I recollect some kind of poster on him, but. . . ." He squinted at the large black man standing in the doorway. "When'd the government start sending blacks into the marshaling business, I'd like to know. Seems to me, fella, I'd better check this out right now. You just stay here, while I get off a telegraph wire to the Feds and check you out. Might be, I should lock you up right now."

One look from the black marshal stopped him in the act of pulling keys from his desk drawer.

"Don't even try it. I'll wait here with the body."

The sheriff could barely bring himself to look away from Moses, but he finally checked out the face of the outlaw. "Yep, looks like the picture of Sorrell to me. Anything in his pockets, any form of identification?"

On the Terror Trail

"Just the fact that he tried to draw on me over at the Golden Rule. That's all I need."

Rifling through the dead man's pockets, the sheriff pulled out some change and a broken bit of pencil. "Might be some more in his saddlebags. Keep your hands out of them, you hear? I don't want you planting evidence or stealing it."

"Hardly, Sheriff. Now, will you please hurry? I've got my own reports to fill out."

Pulling up his suspenders and clapping a beaten hat on his head, the sheriff headed out the door, leaving Moses sitting on a half-log bench along one wall of the jail.

It was always like this, only sometimes worse. Some insisted on locking him up, and he usually consented rather than make it into a fight. Later than sooner, they'd return, with grudging apologies, to let him out after they'd confirmed his position. Some didn't even apologize.

Shoving his brim low over his eyes, Moses tried to force his back to bend to the curves of the plank wall of the jail. Nothing was as good as he'd ever hoped it would be, but then again, it wasn't all bad. Often, there was a substantial reward. Sorrell would probably bring only about two hundred dollars. Yet soon he'd have enough, Moses hoped and prayed. It would all be worth it, when he owned his own land. The night sounds began lulling him to sleep.

Once more he'd add a small amount to the bank balance in St. Louis. But how many more men would he take first, before he got careless? The thought chilled him to the bone, and often he wondered if he didn't already have enough to buy a few acres and some stock. And then he remembered that there wouldn't be anyone to go home to, anyway. He may as well keep building on the dream.

Chapter Two

THE lone light of his small campfire burned in the darkness. Moses pitched camp on the rim, making his own hospitality at the late hour. Pulling out his worn leather volume of poetry by John Keats, he stretched close to his small campfire. Although the gold initials on the spine were becoming cracked and discolored with age and handling, he traced their outline. James Manson Nelson. His books were all that remained, the books they'd studied together, carried with them while catfishing on the Pamunkey River, loaded in the leather-bound trunks they'd carried to the camps of the Confederacy. Now they were Moses' reminders of a dead time, a dead man, a dead civilization.

Reading the poetry aloud, he savored the cadence and passion of the language. Although, if he chose, he could speak as well as any graduate of the University of Virginia, the West was no place for such folderol. Falling asleep with his head on his saddle, the volume tucked against his chest like a lover, Leland Moses dreamed of another world, another time, when he'd been owned by the Nelsons but raised with the family scion like one of their own brood.

He saw, in his dream, the slope of the land, chewed by the cows in summer, down to the muddy banks of the Pamunkey, the oak-fired pattern of the brick on the main house. James and he were running through the tobacco fields, chasing make-believe Indians, boys alive with summer and imagination. Soon, breathless and glistening in the humid heat of August, they'd thrown themselves down beside a rotting log, trying to stifle their giggles with dirty fists.

Then, as they choked back their laughter, a twig beside Jamie's head suddenly twitched, wrapping about his throat tighter than an ascot, tight as the black hand of death, and the boy's face suddenly became that of the young man in the Army camp. Grasping with his fingernails at the head of the asp, Moses struggled in his dream with the beast as Jamie twitched and gasped beneath his hands. Fighting with all his strength as the light grew green and murky with twilight, Moses watched Jamie's face grow black and mottled, like the snake that pinned him by the neck to the soft, mossy ground.

Moses awoke in a sweat, retching for air, his hands numb on the volume of Keats. Diphtheria. Even now, many years later, its memory haunted him, and he could see Jamie dying on that stained Army cot, dying beneath his eyes in a quarantined tent with only his black slave, Leland

Moses, to care for him. Jamie, choking out his last words, freeing his childhood friend. He'd done as Jamie wanted, and had left that night, carrying with him Jamie's fine leather saddlebags filled with the books they'd both loved. Even in death, Jamie had thought of his friend, knowing his freedom lay behind Union lines.

Soft shimmers of predawn light edged the sky. Moses ran a cold hand over his sweaty face, forcing his mind clear of the nightmare. The dream came too quickly when the chase had been hard and the killing quick. Carefully enveloping the Keats in its chamois wrap, he replaced it in the saddlebags. Saddling up, he decided to forgo coffee and ride.

The bay was plain, but sure-footed and fast when speed was essential. Moses hunkered down in the saddle, giving the pack horse a pull to move him out. With a pocket full of Wanted posters, he needed only to reach in and choose his next quarry. A hot breeze blew at his back as he used his rowels on the horse, and he felt relief at moving out into the open again.

Sometimes it worried him that going into a town made his stomach tighten and his hands knot into fists. It wasn't so much what he might have to do as it was the feeling of being bound that towns gave him. Slowing Chloe to a walk, his reins about the saddle horn, he pulled out a handful of posters, studying them carefully. Letting his instincts take over, he decided on the half-Indian, half-Mexican Juan Quanta, who had been rather free with other men's horses and his own bullets. Three men dead, it read on the poster.

"Three men, that's enough for me. What do you think, Chloe?" The bay twitched her ears.

"Let's go north." The sound of his voice was good. Sometimes he didn't speak for days on end, and it felt as if his vocal chords had rusted when he opened his mouth to ask for mail or to order tins of beans and fruit at the dry-goods store. Pulling out his Army compass, he took his bearings. By rough calculation, he determined that it would be about three days before he ran into any sort of town. It would give him time to do some quiet checking at outlying ranches. Chloe's short legs swished through the flatlands, leading him to his next quarry.

After a long day of riding, Moses stopped in the dark. Unsaddling Chloe, he suddenly saw a lone light from a farmhouse flicker in the darkness like a diamond. Moses pitched camp a ways off.

He awoke the next morning, his book resting on his chest, cotton-mouthed from snoring. Stretching, he looked in the direction of the light he'd seen earlier. Time to check out the homestead. Saddling up, he reluctantly decided to forgo coffee, and ride.

There was an air of weary sadness about the little farm. A few peonies struggled out of the yellow dirt edging the front steps. Once it had been a fairly decent house, but now it bore neglect and rapid decline like King Lear's sorrows. Moses noted the faded whitewashed facade, the fallen bars of the remuda, the scruffy chickens scratching in the dirt beside the half-shed.

"Hello, the house." He waited, seated and ready to withdraw if necessary, hand on thigh near his gun.

The leather makeshift hinges of the lone door creaked, and a thin, middle-aged woman emerged, a rifle cradled in her arms.

"Howdy there. What can I do for you?" She showed no surprise at seeing a black man wearing a marshal's badge in her front yard.

"I'd appreciate your taking a look at this poster, ma'am. Name's Moses, Leland Moses." Unfolding the Wanted poster from his vest pocket, he was starting to dismount when a gawky boy, wearing patched britches and an oversized hat, darted out of the half-shed.

"Hold it there, mister. You're in my sights."

"Just a minute here, boy. Hold your horses, I'm a United States Marshal."

The woman rested the rifle against the doorjamb. Nodding to the boy, she strode purposefully to Moses, reaching for the poster.

"Nope, not in my neck of the woods, Marshal. Seeing as how I birth a lot of the babies in these parts, I'd know him if he was a daddy."

Moses believed her. "Well, thanks for your

help. Mind if I water my horse before I move on?"

"Water's God's. You're welcome to all you need."

"Thanks." Dismounting, Moses watched the boy. He hadn't lowered the old shotgun an inch.

"Got a fine boy there, ma'am. A body can't be too careful."

"True, Marshal. Where you heading next?"

"North. I'll find the varmint if he's anywhere in these parts."

"Looks like you've been on the road awhile. No offense, Marshal, but the dust's made you look mighty peculiar."

"No offense taken. Think your boy might be a little less vigilant and lower that weapon? Makes me a little nervous, you might say."

She glanced at his face with direct, kindly eyes. "Suppose so. Tyler, put that away. See if you can get any milk out of Janie for breakfast."

Reluctantly, the boy lowered the shotgun, his thin, hawklike face set in an expression of distrust. "Yes, ma'am."

"I can offer you some biscuits and gravy, if you've time."

Moses was perplexed at her shift. "I'd be grateful. Beans and tinned tomatoes are getting right old. Hot gravy and biscuits sound like heaven."

Nodding abruptly, she gestured for him to tie his horse to her front-porch railing.

On the Terror Trail   17

"Come in. I need a word with you so the boy doesn't hear."

Glancing quickly at the half-shed, he couldn't help but wonder what she had to discuss in private.

The small house was furnished with what had once been fine, stylish rosewood and mahogany pieces. But years and hard use, heat and cold, had taken their toll. Carefully placing his hat on the rack by the door, he stood respectfully in the room, waiting for her to come to the point.

Standing before the old cookstove, she reached for more kindling. "Gracious, where're my manners? Wash bucket's behind the door. Have a seat at the table."

Moses splashed the fresh well water on his hands and face, staring surreptitiously at the woman. She'd shown no surprise, only normal caution, at the appearance of a black man at her front doorstep. Watching her clatter about at the stove, he revised his estimate of her age. Much younger than he'd originally thought, she looked like the once-fine furniture, a refined woman who'd seen too much sun. But the finely drawn lines of her face still showed quality and an Eastern refinement unbowed by the elements.

"Not meaning to pry, ma'am, but you and the boy are a long way from civilization, too long to be alone, the two of you."

Glancing sharply at Moses, she turned back to the stove to lift the tin coffeepot with her apron.

"We do fine, Marshal. But it's the boy I want to talk to you about. You see, he isn't mine. Just showed up, two years ago, on foot, hungry, half crazy. Didn't remember anything about his folks, where he came from, nothing except his name: Tyler. I don't know if he ran off from his folks, if they died, or what. Leastwise, he wasn't from anywhere around here I could determine."

Moses held the rose-painted china cup in his hands, blowing on the hot coffee. "What do you want me to do, Mrs. . .?"

"Sorry, Marshal." Smiling ruefully, she held out a thin, work-hardened hand. "Living out here in the middle of nowhere, I don't get to use my manners much. Hamill's my name, Hope Hamill."

They shook hands, his black fist enveloping her tanned one. She smiled as though it were something she did so seldom that it took thought to add the smile to her eyes. Quickly dropping his hand, she hurried back to the cookstove.

"Gravy's going to burn. Anyway, I was saying about Tyler, the boy. Seeing as how you're traveling in these parts, looking for that wanted man, you might just tack on a few questions, ask if anyone knows of a missing boy. I do some moving about, what with being a midwife, and no one's heard of him, or his family. He's about thirteen now, and if you happen to think on it, I'd appreciate your doing some asking in your marshaling business, sort of official, I guess." She stumbled over the speech as though she were afraid he'd turn down her small request.

"I'd be happy to, Mrs. Hamill. But what'll you do without the boy, if his people come for him?"

"Pack it in, head for town, I guess. Hate to. Jeremiah, my husband, was mighty proud of this place. But there comes a time when we've all got to give up old memories, start new. The boy's all I've got now, but if there's a chance his mama's looking for him, well. . . ."

He liked this woman, worn by adversity but still warm and kind, and willing to give all she had.

Suddenly the boy appeared, his tall frame almost filling the doorway. "Not much this morning, Hope." Stalking to the pine worktable, he plunked down the bucket of milk.

"Take her with you when you go check on the steers, Tyler. See if you can't find some better graze for her."

"Yes, ma'am." Staring hard at Moses, Tyler deliberately sat in the chair at the head of the table.

"Marshal, this is Tyler. Tyler, get your elbows off the table." Mrs. Hamill spooned up the gravy and biscuits, serving them both.

"You been in these parts long?" The boy spooned the gravy into his mouth, his eyes never leaving Moses.

"Been riding awhile. I cover the whole territory, reservation and all. Why do you ask, Tyler?"

"No reason. Just never seen a marshal like you afore."

Moses smiled. "Law's got no color, Tyler."

"I reckon." His eyes, still distrustful, gave Moses another quick appraisal. "But we don't see much of the law, not here."

"Then I guess it's time I did my job, isn't it?"

"Where're you from, Marshal?" Mrs. Hamill, finished serving, sat across from him.

"Back East. Like everyone else." He didn't mean to cut her short, but the last thing he wanted was to discuss his past.

"Yes, like everyone else." For a second, her face was soft and dreamy, as though a sweet memory had replaced the hard reality of the ranch. "Tyler, I won't tell you again, elbows off the table!"

Moses hid a grin behind his spoon as the boy reluctantly obeyed. He'd do as she asked, but knew there was little chance of finding the boy's people. Death was an often and sudden enemy in the territories, and who knew what fever may have struck a lone Conestoga on the prairies. He hoped, for the sake of the kindly woman, that he was right.

Chapter Three

THE Scotsman ran his freckled, stocky fingers through the shock of red hair plastered to his brow with sweat. He hated the heat. With a sigh, he shut his eyes and tried to feel the cool, Scottish breeze blowing off the river, hear the rustle of leaves on the river's edge as he cast his line. He'd never felt water so cold again, no, not in this dry, godforsaken exile in which he'd placed himself.

After all, what he'd done hadn't been all that horrible. But his father, that stern Bible-thumping man, had taken after him like the Red Sea closing in on the Egyptian army. No son of his was going to be a businessman, of all the filthy occupations. That was bad enough. But when his da had found out his "business" had consisted of the sale of some illegal items and a few poached pretties, there'd been the devil to pay. He'd explained, ranting back at his black-frocked patriarch, that he himself hadn't done the stealing, just served as a middleman, like a greengrocer, but there'd been no reasoning. So, accompanied by his father's wrath, and no other memories other than the cool of the Highlands, he'd worked his way to America.

Worked. He chuckled at the memory. Found America ripe for men of cunning and leadership ability, men who weren't afraid to use their wits and their fists when necessary. Of course, the war had made him. Running guns, goods from Europe, pilfered morphine, and raw Scotch whisky, he'd been able to buy and sell men at his bidding like the lord of the manor. Sometimes, he'd say a silent prayer of thanksgiving to his da, the old buzzard, for saving him from a life of pettiness and poverty, compared to what he'd found in his new homeland.

Until that blasted day when Lee had played the last hand at Appomattox Courthouse. Rodney McAlistair had thought he'd go on doing his trading, running his silent little sloops in and out of guarded harbors, but overnight, his status had changed. No longer a hero of sorts, even though he'd been ignored by the society ladies of Charleston in his prime, he found his business drying up, his men arrested and hanged.

"Pshaw!" He spit in the dust of the street, counting the horses switching their tails at flies in front of his saloon. Hadn't taken him long to figure out he'd need to find another war, a small altercation of sorts, to keep his profits growing. Once he'd headed west, it hadn't been hard to track down exactly where his specific talents were marketable and admired. Of course, as he'd grown in stature, it had become easier and easier to buy the sort of men he needed.

That was when he first saw it. His town. Raw, dirty, looking like the wrath of God had spent itself in its imminent demise, he'd felt the vision move him like the power of the Lord that his da had raved on about. This was his promised land. And it hadn't taken him any forty years of wandering in the wilderness to find it, either.

Occasionally, he wondered what had become of his father, preaching his throat raw in the cold stone kirks of the Highlands. The end he envisioned for the self-righteous old man gave him as much pleasure as pressing his Indian slaves' faces in the dirt with the toe of his boot.

Flicking the rivers of sweat from the slope of his clean-shaven jaw, he whistled long and low. Instantly, a small-boned Indian girl appeared behind him on the veranda, her eyes downcast.

"Yes, Mr. McAlistair?" Her inflection had just a hint of the Highlands. He'd taught her himself, from her childhood, when he'd picked her out of the first crop to be sold to the Mexicans.

"Beer, Celinda. And a boy to move the fan."

"Yes, sir." Disappearing on her bare feet into the shadows of the house, she called out for one of the house slaves. Within seconds, a hot breeze settled upon him from the huge palmetto.

The large, frame house was built long and low, much like the weekend homes of the plantation owners in Charleston. McAlistair had remembered every detail of their elegant and cool interiors, the white lace hanging in the long windows built from the ground up, cutting the worst of the sun. Even the green silk swags and oriental carpets had been imported at great cost and no little effort, all in an attempt to mimic a modicum of the elegance and way of life of those rich and arrogant men who had paid through the nose for the goods the blockade-running Scotsman had had for sale. He relished his imitation of their aristocracy, here in the middle of the town he'd called after himself and resurrected from the dead. McAlistair propped himself back on the hand-carved chair, a happy and contented man.

But McAlistair's peaceful moment didn't last. A gathering noise nearby disturbed him, and he sat up with a look of annoyance. A group of his men were gathered by the barn, shouting excitedly.

Built short and square like an Apache, McAlistair shouldered his way through the crowd like a gladiator about to do battle.

"What's going on here?" he demanded. Silence fell over the crowd.

"Nothin', boss." The man who replied was lean and small, like a rat terrier with a nose for fox holes. "Just having us some fun."

The Indian in the center of the circle wiped the blood from his nose. He knew better than to say anything.

"You want fun, you ask me what you can do. Right, Wailes?"

"Sure, anything you say, Mr. McAlistair." With a nod, Wailes sent the crowd scattering. "This here Injun needed a quick lesson, that's all."

"Why?" McAlistair's eyes bored into Wailes. The gunman knew he'd been throwing his weight around more than the little, dark-faced Scotsman liked. No one survived pushing McAlistair around. Circling to the sidewalk, Wailes prowled the perimeter like a cougar sniffing a kill.

"No special reason, boss. Just an Injun. You know."

McAlistair's hand dropped to his gunbelt. Wailes's eyes became slits, although the sun was behind him.

"You don't move a muscle without my say-so. Get saddled. I want you to run an errand for me."

The gunhawk bristled. "I ain't no errand boy. Signed on to do some shooting. This town's deader than a doornail. Ain't had nothing to do for weeks now. Get someone else to run your errands." Spitting out the words, Wailes felt the tingling sensation in his hands that meant he was ready. *About time,* he thought. Injun, McAlistair, didn't matter whom he killed, he was ready for blood.

The Winchester cracked from an upstairs window. Spinning with the impact, Wailes felt a slight moment of surprise before he hit the street, face down. He hadn't heard a sound.

McAlistair kicked Wailes's gun from his holster and hoisted it up. Flipping it casually, he signaled to his backshooter. The crowd had scattered for shelter at the first move.

"Anyone else want to run an errand for me?" His low, thickly accented voice carried like a bullet through clouds.

"Sure, boss, where you need it run?" A gangly boy of about sixteen inched his way from behind a pillar. His poorly cut hair was hanging in his eyes, and he shoved at it with hands cracked from tilling the earth.

"You new, boy?" McAlistair stuck the .45 in his belt, and sized up the new kid.

"Yessir, guess so. Just got here, that is."

"Got a gun?"

"Nope. Leastwise, not yet. But I know how to shoot."

Tossing the .45 to the kid, McAlistair watched him fumble for the weapon. "We'll see about that. You make a mistake, kid, and you're dead. Still want to run my errands?"

"Sure." Grinning, the kid jabbed the gun in his belt and pulled on a greasy old hat.

"There's a man named Thomas Two Hats, out by Twin Bluffs. Hasn't paid me my money this month. See that I have it by tonight. I'll be waiting."

The kid stared at McAlistair's back as he

pushed into the saloon. "But, Mr. McAlistair, what if he ain't got it?"

McAlistair never turned, his hands still on the saloon door. "I only give orders once, kid."

The boy heard the ice in the brogue, and knew he was in trouble.

McAlistair smiled. "Now get moving. I want my money."

Chapter Four

H E knew the town was trouble from a mile away. Dusty even at that distance, its false facades jagged against the bright blue of the sky at awkward angles. Tying Chloe to a railing at the Mercantile, Moses rinsed his hands in the horse trough. Strange, he thought, there were more whites than Indians on the street. Most towns were Indian owned and run.

Searching for the sure sign of justice, he found a large white oak near the middle of the rows of buildings. Striding over to its bullet-pocked bark, he fingered the holes as he watched for the local law. Sure enough, he'd attracted the attention of the man.

A big half-Cherokee, gut spilling over his belt, grease staining his faded red shirt, watched Moses. The marshal stared at the man squarely.

"You the law around here?" Moses called out as he mounted the steps to the small jail.

"Who wants to know?" The man spat in the dust at Moses' feet.

Pulling out the poster with his authority papers, Moses showed his badge in his palm. The

Indian glanced contemptuously at the silver metal against the paleness of the black man's fingers.

"Federal. Looking for this man." Moses repocketed the sign of his position.

"Don't bother. No one here you'd be interested in."

Moses watched the slow traffic in the shabby little town. Too few men were dressed in the work clothes of farmers, too many sidearms were tied low and ready. "You sure about that?" His voice was tight. He'd seen towns like this before, havens for dangerous trash of all kinds.

"Don't push me while I'm educating you as to the facts of life in my town, Marshal."

The sheriff sucked in his gut and turned to walk away. Then he added, "You might as well know this town's owned by a man named McAlistair, and you'd do well to stay outta his way. I can guarantee he won't like you. You'll end up at the barber's getting prettied up for a funeral. Your own."

Moses blocked his path with a boot.

Blustering, the gunman's hand dropped halfway to his sidearm. "Careful," he snarled. "We've got our own ways of handling troublemakers from Washington. Looks to me like you're aching to make some mischief."

"I'm the law out here, and don't you forget it. I'll do my job whether you like it or not." Jamming the poster back in his pocket, Moses turned on his heel.

Since he didn't want to tread just yet on the vipers he knew were curled in the saloon, he searched the street for an eating establishment. News of who was traveling through places like this usually passed through the local café right after it hit the saloon.

Moses found a cracked, peeling sign reading *Wynoma's*. Vertical boards, sun-faded and chinked with clay, covered the log building. The smell of hot apples and cinnamon wafted past the gingham curtain covering the kitchen door. Dropping his battered hat on a pine table, he headed for the origin of the aroma.

"Can I get some of that apple pie?" Expecting to find an Indian, he stopped in surprise at the sight of the woman rolling biscuits. Tall, thin, dressed in a faded blue calico dress with a clean white apron, she laid aside the rolling pin as he stepped into her kitchen.

"Be with you momentarily. Want coffee to go with the pie?"

He couldn't help but stare at her deep, dark skin and high cheeks. Black women were few and far between, except in the areas where the tribes had freed their slaves and given them land to plant cotton, keeping them on as sharecroppers.

"Yes, ma'am. Don't mean to bother you. I can wait."

Her eyes bored into his. "No bother. Customer's always welcome."

He backed out of the kitchen, suddenly awkward. Seating himself at the pine table, he straightened his bandanna. She was out of the kitchen within seconds, coffeepot in one hand, a plate heaped high with apple pie in the other.

"I'll get you a cup. Want sugar for your pie?"

"You must be a Southerner, ma'am. Only people I ever knew sprinkled sugar on a pie smelling as sweet as that come from Georgia."

"South Carolina. Now what else can I get you?" She returned with the plain white china mug and a fork. Standing with hands on hips, she watched him unsmilingly.

"You could sit a spell."

"No time for that. Got biscuits in the oven."

"Well, soon as they're out, then. I'd appreciate it if we could talk some."

"Now look here, mister. Just because you're black as me doesn't mean I've got to entertain you. I've got a business to run."

Scraping back the chair, Moses stood. "Sorry. Didn't properly introduce myself. Name's Moses, Leland Moses. Federal Marshal. Looking for some information, that's all."

Softening, she looked back at the kitchen, then shrugged.

"Mine's Wynoma Webster. Biscuits'll take a few more minutes, I suppose."

He held a chair for her. "Join me. I'd be honored."

Smiling, she sat wearily. "Been on my feet all day, doing the baking. How's the pie?"

Moses quickly shoveled a forkful in his mouth. "Best I ever ate. God's truth."

"All that flattery—you've got to be from the South yourself, Mr. Marshal."

"Yep." His tone stopped that line of conversation. "I've already had the dubious honor of meeting your local lawman. On first impression, I'd say he's less than vigorous in upholding any sort of peace around here." He paused. "If I offend you, Mrs. Webster, let me know."

"Nothing you can say about the sheriff can offend me. This town's owned and run by one man, and the law can't do a durned thing about it, Federal Marshal or not. Sheriff's his man, does what the boss wants and nothing else. Mind you, Mr. McAlistair doesn't take too kindly to any authority but his own in these parts. You plan on staying long around here?"

"Long enough to find this fellow." Unfolding the grimy Wanted poster, he watched her face as she studied the picture.

"I don't read much. What's his name?"

"Juan Quanta. Ever seen him?"

Her dark eyes squinted as she traced the outline of the sketch. "Kinda hard to tell. This isn't much of a likeness of anyone I know of. But the name rings a bell."

On the Terror Trail 33

"Many Mexican types come through here?"

"Sure, lots. This town's about the only place they can rest up and stock up, afore heading back with the Indians they've captured. No one to stop them, not in McAlistair, with Mr. McAlistair getting a cut when the slaves are sold at the border." Her face saddened, and she continued, "Wish there was something I could do, but I've gotta keep low around here, since I make most of my living serving them food."

"I understand." Moses ducked his head, forking in a piece of pie. "Mighty fine pie, Mrs. Webster. Just fine."

"Call me Wynoma. Everyone else does." She stood, tightening the bow on her apron. "Back to work. Can't sit around all day gossiping." She turned for her kitchen.

"Marshal." She paused. "I'd appreciate it if you didn't say I'd discussed your poster. Black folks keep pretty low in these parts, seeing as how most of them were freed from the tribes with the war and all. Some of the Indians didn't want to do it, but some black folks, like me, we got tribal rights now, and I don't want to do nothing to rock the boat. Got me a good living here, what with the restaurant and doing midwifing. Please?"

"Of course." He gave her a smile. "Far as I'm concerned, all I got here was some pie and coffee."

Looking relieved, she turned again for her biscuits.

"Just one more thing. You know a lady name of Hope, I believe it's Hamill? Got a boy called Tyler living with her?"

"Sure do. We two, we do all the birthings around here. She does the white ladies, and I take everything else. We've been friends a long time. She came out here to missionary, married a half-Indian. Good man, but he died. She got to keep their place, seeing as how her man was one of the tribes'. But times are right hard for her, so I keep telling her to move on into town, set up a dressmaking shop, or come cook with me. It's too hard on a woman out there all alone."

Moses was taken aback. "She's got the boy."

"Boy can't protect a woman alone when she needs protecting. 'Sides, the boy isn't quite right. She's done all she can to give him a good, loving home. What you want to know about her?"

"Well, I was just out that way, and she asked me to make inquiries about the boy. See if I can find his family."

"She's been doing that since he wandered in, all sick and feverish and half crazy. That boy's all she has, and it'd kill her if he ever took off. So don't you pay her no never-mind—there's no way on earth his folks are alive. Probably some brave running south of the border has their scalps on his lance." Pushing at her hair with the back of her wrist, she gave him a hard stare. "Don't you go doing anything that'll hurt that woman, Marshal Moses. Cause I'd take it right personal."

Watching her retreat to the gingham-covered door, he wondered at the friendship of the white farm woman and the black cook. If he had more time, he'd have liked to talk a while longer with Wynoma Webster.

Finishing the pie and coffee, he paid his bill with coins on the table. Time to get on with the business of Juan Quanta. Chatting with Wynoma was too pleasant a possibility; it could interfere with his real mission. Mr. McAlistair or not, he'd get his man.

After stabling Chloe, Moses settled down to watch the movement on the street for a while. Half hidden by the shadow of the Mercantile's porch, he tipped his hat over his face and pretended to doze on the rough plank bench. The heat of the day had driven most of the men into the saloon. Ignoring the marshal, the sheriff had disappeared into his slovenly jail.

He'd have bet his bottom dollar every man on the street was on a Wanted poster, or should be. Few paid him any attention, assuming he was one of the local blacks freed from the tribes. At least, that was the only explanation he could come up with for the fact that he was being so totally ignored.

Indians delivering goods, hauling freight, seemed oblivious to the riffraff. Moses wondered what had happened, since towns in the territory were run by tribal courts, which had more law and order than most he'd seen. He'd known of a man, convicted by the tribal court of murder and sentenced to die, who'd been allowed to go home to bring in the crops, with the promise he'd appear at the death tree on the appointed day. Sure enough, the man had ridden into town a month later and taken his position to be shot. Assessing the situation in McAlistair made it obvious something had gone askew.

His stomach began grumbling about sundown. Tired and sore from the hard bench, Moses considered taking some tins from his saddlebags and making a quick meal of it. But the thought of apple pie at Wynoma's was too tempting. It had been ages since he'd eaten a real home-cooked dinner, and the idea of seeing the woman gnawed at him like a longing for sweets. So far his lookout had been fruitless. Knowing he'd have to face the lions in their den before long, he gave in to the craving for a little taste of civilization first.

An Indian couple and some lone men wearing low-slung gunbelts were the first customers. Assuming an air of deference, Moses doffed his hat and headed for the kitchen. A young Indian girl was loading a tray. Whirling with her arms full, she almost collided with him head-on.

"Just a minute, mister. Miss Wynoma don't allow no one in her kitchen, so you just take a seat, and I'll be out in a minute."

On the Terror Trail 37

Wynoma dropped the iron lid back on the cookstove. "Who's that, Vera?"

"Nobody, Miss Wynoma—just some man."

"Sorry to be bothering you again, Wynoma." Moses pulled the gingham curtain shut behind him. "Thought I'd come get another piece of that pie, if there's any left."

He could have sworn she darkened as she twirled to stare at him. "Ain't you got no sense? What you doing back here? Thought you'd have figured out things by now and gotten yourself out of town."

He watched the Indian girl, frowning at Wynoma's recognition of him.

"Vera, get out there. I'll take care of him."

"Yes, ma'am." Reluctantly backing through the door, Vera gave him a hard look.

"Didn't mean to startle you. It's just that, well, I was hoping for a home-cooked dinner and some conversation for a change."

Clanging pots to hide their voices, Wynoma gestured for him to move out of the doorway. "I've been hearing about you, Marshal. See those two types by the door? Seems the sheriff let it be known you're out looking, and the word's spread faster than the plague over Egypt. You been sitting right on Main Street all day, asking for trouble."

He chuckled. "Guess so. Must admit, it's kind of surprising something hasn't cut loose by now.

Suppose I'll have to do some kicking around in the cow pies to find the real manure."

"Just don't you go doing any of that in my place, if you please. Don't need no bullet holes in my cookstove, thank you kindly." She served a plate with steak and fried eggs, fresh corn and biscuit. "Those types by the door, they know Quanta. Told you I recognized the name. He's one of McAlistair's Indian hunters. Don't see him in town too often. Mostly he's running the ones he captures south of the border. Sells them to the Mexicans for McAlistair."

Instinctively, Moses pushed his back against the wall and checked the door. Holding aside the curtain, he assessed the two men Wynoma had pointed out. "A whole different ball of wax than some horse thieving. Guess his new line of business doesn't matter as much as some horseflesh. Where's he now?"

Exasperated, Wynoma poured coffee into cups. "Don't you listen too good? I told you, he's one of McAlistair's. That means you aren't worth these coffee grounds after tonight if you expect to go finding Quanta."

It had always been this way. Once he'd decided to find a certain man and bring him in, nothing could deter him from finding the trail, no matter how cold it might be by the time he got there. Checking his gun, he put his finger to his lips. "Shh. Just go on with what you're doing—pre-

On the Terror Trail 39

tend I've lit out the back door. I'll wait for them to leave, then follow 'em."

For a second, she looked frightened. "You're loco, I knew it." The smell of burning meat pulled her attention back to the stove. "Why I ever said anything to you in the first place is beyond me. I should have known better, I swear it."

Grinning at her self-chastisement, he pulled open the door of the pie safe and took his position behind it. Anyone looking into the kitchen from the dining room would see just the pie safe, its punched-tin door ajar.

"Don't say anything else. Tell Vera I left."

Just then Vera stalked through the doorway. "Need some butter for the biscuits." She glanced quickly around the kitchen. "What happened to that man?"

"Nothing," Wynoma snapped, spooning a wad of soft butter on a plate. "Left the back way. He was just asking for some handouts. Threw him out. Now get back out there."

Taking one last quick glance around, Vera sashayed back to the diners. "Sure hope so. Looked like trouble to me," was her parting shot.

"I have lost my ever-loving mind," Wynoma mumbled.

The smells of hot, fresh food lulled Moses for a while. Then, it seemed like hours later, Vera hauled her last tray of dirty dishes into the kitchen. "Them two by the door, they say they're waiting for someone. Don't want nothing more to eat, but it sure looks funny. Like trouble, if you ask me."

Wynoma glanced quickly at the door. "Tell them to go. We gotta wash up."

Vera spoke with the men. Shaking their heads, they stood. Gesturing angrily, Vera tried to wave them through the front door. Suddenly, one of the men grabbed her arm, swinging her to one side. Stumbling, she fell to the floor.

"Miss Wynoma, watch out!" Shouting, Vera struggled to her feet.

Whipping out a gun, the man held it to her face. "Another word and you're dead."

Moses knew instantly what was happening. Holding his finger to his lips, he signaled for Wynoma to move away from the gingham door. She hid a kitchen knife under her apron as she slid quietly behind the pie safe.

Sliding out his gun, Moses held it ready. Still hidden, he called out, "You out there! Let the women go. This is between us."

Grinning, the man with the gun drawn on Vera hauled her to her feet beside him. "Sure. Just come on out. We got some talking to do, Mr. Lawman."

"He's got a gun!" Vera screamed. Smacking her, the gunman threw the girl aside.

"You got five seconds, and she's dead. Throw out your gun." Like sandpaper, the rough edge of his voice bit into the wood of Moses' fear. Harming innocent bystanders had long been his

On the Terror Trail 41

nightmare, one that tormented him almost as much as the dream of Jamie's death.

Wynoma stared at him, her eyes heavy and leaden. "Looks like they've got you but good, Marshal. You have another gun?"

"Rifle, with my gear at the livery. That's all."

"I'll be back." Slipping out the back door, Wynoma edged away into the darkness.

Trying to buy some time, Moses called out, "What kind of guarantee can you give me you'll let the girl go if I come out?"

"Listen to them fancy words. How do you like that, Jimmy? Guarantee? I'll show you guarantee." Blasting away at the kitchen, the gunman kicked over a table, dropping behind it. Dragging Vera by the neck, the other man did the same.

"Hold it. Don't hurt the girl." Throwing out the Colt, Moses waited a second. "I'll come out as soon as you let her go."

"You ain't got too much to bargain with, Mr. Marshal. Now get your tail out here. We got a man wants to have a discussion with you, and he's been waiting long enough."

Edging around the door, Moses saw Vera crawl toward the kitchen. "No, go the other way, get out front," he hissed. Angry at his own stupidity in placing the women in jeopardy and not getting out of there earlier, he watched Vera stumble out the front door.

"So who wants to see me? Seems you could

have issued a friendlier invitation. Always ready to do some palavering."

"Shaddup." Kicking away the Colt, the gunman jabbed his weapon in Moses' side. "Come on, Lawman, we got an appointment. Now move it."

Tripping over the fallen tables, Moses slowed down the pace of the march out the door. He wondered what Wynoma planned to do if she could find the rifle hidden in his gear, but he held little hope. After all, they'd only just met, and she didn't owe him anything.

The dim light of the room behind the saloon shadowed most of the faces. Leaning against the rough wood walls, one by one the men pulled their weapons as he was shoved and tied into a chair. The sheriff unpeeled his behind from a bench, hitching up his pants.

"Told you to stay out of McAlistair, didn't I? Well, let me introduce Mr. McAlistair." His oily voice oozed with the pride of a bully showing off a prize rattler.

McAlistair stepped out of the shadows into the full light of the lantern. "Hear tell you're asking about a man named Quanta. Why?"

Clearing his throat, Moses assessed the situation as not only bad, but desperate. If he made it out alive, it would be a miracle. "Got a wanted on him—horse thieving, murder."

"Well, I do declare, now, Marshal, I've known Juan Quanta a long time, and the truth is, he ain't

On the Terror Trail

that kind of man at all. So why don't you just ride on out of here, peaceable like, and forget all about Juan." McAlistair's voice bit through the smoke of the lantern like steel.

Moses considered his options. But something about a man like McAlistair bit into his craw like the strangle of diphtheria.

"You seem to be forgetting, McAlistair, I'm a Federal Marshal. I'm the law around here."

Hoots and guffaws greeted his announcement. Sputtering with amusement, McAlistair stuck his freckled face, surrounded by greasy hair, into Moses' face. "I'm the law in McAlistair, Mr. Federal Marshal, and don't you forget it." Moses placed his accent as Scots. Whipping out a small knife, McAlistair poked its point into Moses' throat. "Now are you going to forget all about Quanta, or do you want to die?"

Biting back his response, Moses saw the blood rising in their eyes. "Sure, I'll forget about Quanta. All you had to do was ask."

The bloodlust rose in them at his answer. *Lord, have mercy,* he thought. *I've done it now.* Twisting at the rawhide thongs wrapped about his wrists, he got ready to dodge the expected blows. The gun butt that slashed behind his ear crashed him into the table with the lamp, sending glass and hot oil everywhere. He never heard the stomping feet that broke his ribs.

Chapter Five

Quanta threw the reins at the blacksmith. "Back left, lost a shoe." The Indian nodded and put down the wagon trace he'd been mending. He knew Quanta, McAlistair's chief slave-runner. Avoiding Quanta's narrow eyes, the smithy led the horse to the post.

"Ready in about an hour." The evil eye followed Quanta's stare like crows after newly planted seed, and the smithy knew better than to risk a glance at the back of the gunman as he strode into the hot sun. The last man to get a full load of Quanta's expressionless eyes had died under a stampeded wagon just a few days later. Muttering a sacred charm under his breath, the Indian braced the gelding's hoof between his knees to measure the shoe.

Blasted Indian! Quanta thought. *Stupid, ignorant savages, all of them.* Beating at the dust on his hat, he ran a quick hand over his grimy, pockmarked face. No time for cleaning up, but who cared, anyway? Certainly not Rodney McAlistair.

Jamming his straight black hair under the

Mexican hat, Quanta kicked the road dirt off his spurs on the rough planks of the walk. Three Anglo gunmen lolled back in chairs in front of McAlistair's office.

"He in?"

One of the Anglos opened his pale brown eyes to stare at the gunman asking the question. Quanta didn't recognize the kid, his face as hungry looking as a mongrel dog's. Kicking the chair out from under the boy, Quanta's hand was already on his gun before the kid could scramble to his feet, his face splotched with rage.

"Go tell him Quanta's here." Snarling the words, Quanta checked to make sure the other two stayed out of it. They leaned back, unconcerned with the gunplay about to burst out.

The kid had finally seen Quanta's hand. As he stumbled to his feet, his eyes never left Quanta's hip. Shoving aside the door, he backed through it, hatred making his gait stiff and stiltlike. Quanta could hear him spit out the name at the clerk who kept McAlistair's accounts.

"Well, show him in, you idiot."

Quanta waited a fraction of a second for the tow-headed kid to step aside. When he didn't move fast enough, the gunman whipped out his pistol and jammed the barrel against the boy's solar plexus.

"Move when I'm around, understand, *muchacho?*" Quanta's face was like stone, his eyes cold with contempt.

Sagging against the wall, the boy stared at him, his hands twitching nervously at his sides. Quanta holstered the weapon, turning on his high Mexican heels as he did so. The kid would be dead before the month was out, if he lasted that long.

"You taking all comers these days?" Quanta dropped his hat on the cowhide-upholstered chair and edged clear of the back window of McAlistair's office. Thumbs tucked in his gunbelt, he propped himself against the wall and waited for McAlistair to look up from the ledgers spread on his desk like huge death certificates.

"They weed themselves out. Like I always say, scum rises to the top." Closing the sterling-silver inkwell, McAlistair tapped his pen on the blotter to clear its reserves.

Quanta knew just how far he could go with the man who paid for his services. "One out there's about to sink fast."

McAlistair laughed, spreading his pink freckled hands wide on the edge of the desk. "About time you came to see me, my good man. I've been missing your dour sense of humor these hot days." Standing, McAlistair stomped to shake his pants clear of his boot tops. "And I imagine you'd like your pay."

The two men were suddenly without smiles. Pulling a leather pouch from inside his shirt, Quanta tossed it on the desk. "My cut's five hundred dollars." Watching McAlistair spread the gold from the bag on the desk like poker chips, Quanta resisted the urge to speak. He already knew what McAlistair was going to say.

"Not such a good haul this time, laddie. What happened?"

Quanta's black eyes burned into McAlistair. "You know what happened." He hated the Scotsman's games.

McAlistair leaned back like a fisherman about to reel in a big one. "Well, why don't you tell me your side of it? Shall we say, just for the record?" His eyes were as cold as those of his hired killer.

Quanta's lids lowered to slits. "There was some trouble at the border. Nothing I couldn't handle, but some of the squaws got hit. That's all."

"If that's all, why weren't you ready to handle a spot o' trouble without damaging my merchandise?" McAlistair brought his opened palms down on the edge of the desk like a preacher leaning into the pulpit to admonish a congregation of lost souls. "I'll tell you why, *my* good man," he said coolly, emphasizing the possessive "my." McAlistair's hands dropped to his lap as he sat again behind the desk. Quanta shifted his thumbs closer to his guns.

"You were chewing those little pills again, weren't you, Quanta? A bit groggy, not quite awake when you got jumped, my guess would be." The lilt left his voice, and it became hard and flat. "I've warned you once before: I don't give a tinker's diddle what you do on your own time, but you keep a clear head when you're working for me, blast you!"

Quanta's jaw tightened. His eyes never left McAlistair's. One shift, one slight twitch of the Scotsman's muscles, and Quanta would kill him. Both men knew it. And both knew that afterward Quanta would never get out of town alive.

"You keep your mind on business, my friend, and not in dreamland. I can't be affording these kinds of mistakes. My competition will start thinking I'm slipping, and next thing you know, they'll be poaching on my preserves!" Counting out the gold, McAlistair shoved a small pile across to Quanta. "Well, laddie, now that we've concluded our business, shall we have a drink? A spot of tequila, eh?"

Slithering to the desk, the gunman snatched the coins and stuffed them in the empty pouch. "Not this time. Business first." It wouldn't be long before he ran his own show, with his own string of *pistoleros,* men who could set up a slave-running operation that would put McAlistair's operation to shame. Quanta was going to give McAlistair a taste of what was to come.

The Scotsman waited for Quanta to leave the office, the Spanish spurs jangling in the silence. Everyone had heard the tongue-lashing, just as he'd planned. Now he waited for the results he knew were coming.

Quanta patted his pocket that held the few

On the Terror Trail 49

peyote buttons he had left. "You, boy," he snarled at the green kid he'd bullied earlier. "Fetch me the Injun at the saloon, the one who swabs the floors, now!"

The young *pistolero* had been waiting. "Get him yourself. I work for Mr. McAlistair, not you," he spit back. This time he was already on his feet, his hand hovering by his gun.

Quanta slid a cheroot from his front shirt pocket, slowly lifting it to his lips as the kid's eyes followed the smoke. Before the boy knew what happened, Quanta bent and fired from the hip, the movement one quick blur as the kid crumpled like dirty laundry.

"Aw, Juan, no fair. You shoulda given us a bit more sport here, fella. That was much too easy." McAlistair's brogue teased the gunman. Striding to Quanta, McAlistair clapped him on the shoulder. "Now, how about that drink?"

Quanta's anger had dissipated like smoke in the wind the moment he'd felt his finger on the trigger. McAlistair might not have known it, but he was the one who lay dead in the hot sun; it was his florid face that sagged in the dirt, not the kid's.

The two men, one plump and red-haired, the other thin and dark like a well-used whip, strode to the saloon, the body of the dead errand boy forgotten. Quanta had, for a while, satisfied his craving for revenge on the man who dared to criticize him. Little did he know that the wily foreigner had ordered the green gunman to stand guard that day, setting him up as a sacrificial lamb to appease the bitterness he knew would erupt in his top gun. He needed Quanta a while longer, but the day would soon arrive when the man would be an unnecessary annoyance.

"First round on me, my man." Laughing loudly, McAlistair clapped the gunfighter on the shoulder.

Quanta slinked sideways like a rattler evading the hooves of a slashing horse. McAlistair's raucous bray ceased abruptly.

Quanta left town as quickly as he'd slithered in. The smithy once more evaded his eyes and made the signs to ward off evil as the gunman spurred down the street.

Chapter Six

EACH jolt of the spear in his side threatened to drag Moses out of the darkness. Groaning, he struggled to stay deep in the oblivion protecting him from more agony, but found his eyes open, seeing only blackness.

"Lord, where am I?" His throat was raspy and tight with the effort of breathing.

"Shh," a voice replied, as he felt a soft hand cover his lips. "We're not out of town yet."

"Why can't I see anything?" he mumbled through her fingers.

"I told you, hush now, so hush. It's dark, that's why. We're going to get you out of here so no one can see."

The kitchen smell of her apron, which was folded beneath his head, told him her identity.

"Wynoma? Where'd you find me?"

"Out back of the livery. McAlistair's men dumped you there when they got through using you for fun. You don't look so handsome now, Marshal."

He tried to grin at her evaluation of his looks. "Glad you think I'm handsome."

Her hand pressed tightly about his mouth. "Be still, you fool. Listen to me, just for once."

Acquiescing, he concentrated on assessing the damage to his anatomy. Dried blood caked his face, but there was no real damage, except to his ribcage. Hot knives drove into his lungs with every breath. The bones would take a while to heal, time he didn't have if he was to get Quanta. McAlistair's desire to rid himself of the law had nothing to do with one outlaw, but with what the outlaw was doing for the boss.

"Where are we going?" he asked finally, sure they'd cleared town. The stars were so close in the velvet smoothness of the sky he wanted to reach out and touch one, but pain kept him still.

"Miss Hope's place. You'll be safe there until you mend. Folks don't go out her way much."

"And you? What's going to happen when they find out you got me out of town?"

"They'll never know. For all anyone'll suspect, I'm out doing a birthing. Woman out this way is expecting any day now, and I usually go sit a spell ahead of time with her, so there's no need to fetch me. Vera runs the place without me, and she'll keep her mouth shut. She don't like McAlistair any more than most Indians." He felt her place a cool palm on his head.

"Don't feel like you're fixing to get fever, so I reckon they didn't hurt none of your vitals. Thought for sure you were a goner when they

On the Terror Trail 53

hauled you out of there by the heels. By the way, where'd you hide that rifle? Never did find it."

He laughed, and ended up coughing painfully instead. "Wrapped in canvas, under the manure pile. Should have told you, but I was busy doing other things at the time."

"Well, I got your bags and told Vera to find a boy to ride out on the horse. That'll throw them off for a while, since they'll figure you decided to pack it in and quit. But I mean it, Leland Moses, you better get your hide out of here soon as you're able. Next time, they'll kill you for sure."

Rocking along on the tail of the wagon, he considered her words. Knowing she was right, he was briefly tempted to pack it in and head out for another man. Heaven knew, there were plenty to choose from. But there was more going on than he was willing to walk away from, and his battered sides had a lot to do with it. No man should kick another while he was down, and he was going to make sure McAlistair learned that lesson.

"Hmm," he replied, studying the stars. "How much farther in this feather bed?"

"Just be grateful it isn't the undertaker's board, and quit your complaining. I always did mean to grease that squeak."

He hesitated briefly. "Why me, Wynoma? No matter what you say, you've got to live in McAlistair. If they find out, you're going to wake up one morning to find your café burned to the ground."

He heard her slap the rump of the mule with the reins. "Guess there's a lot of reasons. Don't like McAlistair and his riffraff. Folks ignore what's going on, but I can't. Those Indians, just because they're not white, they don't deserve getting sold, no more than you or me. I'm free now, so I know what losing it means, more than if I'd never had it. And I suppose you aren't such a bad lawman, even if you are awful stupid. Leastwise, you wanted to help Miss Hope find the boy's folks, and I admire that. Not many take time to go out of their way on business that's not theirs."

She cleared her throat and sighed. "Guess I did some fibbing to you too. That man you're looking for, that Quanta, came to town. He's one of McAlistair's slave-runners. Left a while afore you got beat up, though. Just wanted you to know."

Wishing he could see her face, he longed for the knowledge of her that could come only with the years. "Thank you," was his simple reply. Speech was becoming harder as his ribs screamed loudly with pain. Concentrating on the waves that washed over him with the movement of the wagon, he tried to suppress his desire to ask her more. There'd be time later, he hoped. Time after he'd found Quanta and taught McAlistair the lesson he had coming.

Dawn was just breaking its pale lilac and orange streaks on the horizon when they pulled into the Hamill homestead. Wynoma climbed down from the wagon, reaching to touch his face before she left. "You awake?"

"Am now." He forced out the words.

"I'll get Hope and the boy to come help get you out of here. Figure you've stiffened right up. Don't worry, soon as I get you bandaged and get a stiff belt of laudanum down your throat, you'll be out like a light. Nothing like sleep to cure what ails you."

"No laudanum." Grasping the edge of the wagon bed, he tried pulling himself upright. "Aargh!" Collapsing back, Moses clutched the rough wood planks with his nails, waiting for the agony to subside.

"Hold still, for Pete's sake!" Mumbling to herself, Wynoma marched to the front porch of the house. "Men, they never do listen to nothin' a woman tells 'em. Why I'm bothering is almost beyond me. Hope, you up yet? It's me, Wynoma. Hope?"

Moses could hear no response. Rapping on the door, Wynoma called out again. The lack of an answer didn't worry her. After all, Hope could be out midwifing. Pushing at the door's weak leather hinges, Wynoma started to stride through when the stench stopped her. "Oh, dear heaven. . . ."

Moses heard her. "What is it?" Worried at the fear in her voice, he tried once more to sit up, this time succeeding despite the pain. "Wynoma?" Although weak and unable to stand, he knew something was very wrong. "Wynoma, what's the matter?"

Wynoma waved at the flies gathering in the congealed blood. "Tyler, Tyler, talk to me."

The boy crouched by the woman's body, his knees under his chin, hands locked around them, knuckles white. His face was caked in dried blood. Pushing away his hair, Wynoma felt the wound with her fingers, trying to keep her eyes from Hope Hamill.

"Tyler, come outside, boy. It's me, Wynoma. I'm not going to hurt you. Come on, stand up there, boy." Pulling at his hand, she tried to get him on his feet. Refusing to meet her gaze, the boy continued rocking back and forth.

"What happened, Tyler? Can you tell me that much?" Shaking her head, Wynoma surveyed the chaos in the house. Hope Hamill had put up a fight, or whoever had slit her throat had gone on a spree of slashing and destruction. Knife marks scarred the surface of even the lintel over the fireplace, as though the murderer wanted to leave his mark for all posterity to see.

Forcing herself to look directly at her friend, the black woman leaned over to close the eyes.

"No," the boy cried. "Don't do that! She can't see with her eyes closed!" Fighting Wynoma's encircling arms, he tried to reach the dead woman. "She's got to see morning come!"

"No, Tyler, it's over. She can't see no more." Pulling him out the door, she dragged him into the yard. "Don't fight me, Tyler. It's Wynoma . . . remember me, Wynoma?" Sure he'd lost his mind, she repeated the name in a reassuring voice.

Suddenly he stopped struggling. "Wynoma, he came. Killed her, thought he'd killed me. Didn't . . . can't. I'm going to find him, make him pay for what he did to her. . . ." Sobbing, he collapsed into her arms.

"Hush, Tyler, I'm here," Wynoma crooned. "It'll be fine—I'll take care of you, just come on with me," she murmured, edging him farther into the yard. She suddenly couldn't stand the stench of death a moment longer. Whatever the boy had witnessed, it would take a while to get him to tell the story.

As he inched himself out of the wagon Moses had heard the wild sobbing from the house. "Wynoma?" he croaked, the effort causing him to double over and clutch his shattered ribs. Even in the midst of the searing pain, he assessed the situation. No chickens scratched in the dirt, the door to the cow shed stood raggedly ajar, no smoke came from the chimney. Either Mrs. Hamill had pulled out, or death had come first. Forcing himself upright, Moses checked the ammunition in the rifle Wynoma had packed in the wagon. Old, with a cracked stock, it was still better than nothing. Working the lever, he edged around the wagon and tried to walk steadily across the yard.

"Wynoma, are you all right?" He tried once more. "What's happened? Mrs. Hamill?"

Wynoma held the weeping boy engulfed in her long arms like a rag doll. Dragging him toward Moses, she crooned, "Tyler, Tyler, listen to me. Get in the wagon. I'll take care of everything. Don't you worry now, just come along."

Seeing the stricken expression on Wynoma's face, Moses knew his intuition had been correct. It was death. "How did it happen?"

Wynoma stared at him with hollow eyes. "Don't say nothing in front of the boy. Got to find a shovel, get her buried soon as we can." Pulling out the blanket she'd laid over Moses, she wrapped it about the ice-cold boy. "Tyler, lie down. I'll be right back, I promise."

With wooden eyes, Tyler followed Wynoma back to the house. Hobbling behind her, Moses could smell the destruction of human flesh. He was unprepared for the sight of the house, however. Sudden fever, illness, often struck down settlers. But the wanton destruction of the house and the woman was out of the pattern of death as he'd seen it. Even Kiowas, as he remembered them from his cavalry days, would have been more methodical in their killing and pillaging. What had happened at the Hamill place was nothing more than rage out of control. Finding the woman's shawl still on a peg behind the door, Moses laid it over her mutilated face.

"Tyler, take Miss Wynoma to the wagon." Speaking gently to the boy, Moses gestured for Wynoma to take him. Swallowing hard, her eyes wet with tears, she nodded and once more took Tyler in her arms.

"Tyler, the marshal's going to take care of everything. Just you and me, let's go sit down together, and you try to tell me everything." Steering him once more away from the devastation, Wynoma glanced back at Moses with sudden, fierce anger. "You'll take care of everything, won't you? You'll find out who did this, right, Marshal?"

Nodding, Moses silently cursed the day he'd chosen Quanta for his prey. If he hadn't, he'd never have met Hope Hamill. And that meant he'd never have seen her dead. It was a sight he wasn't going to soon forget.

Chapter Seven

QUANTA slashed at the rump of the horse with his knotted quirt. Spitting obscenities at the Indians tied to the backs of the pack horses, he spurred forward. It had taken too much time to kill the woman. He had to make his delivery promptly or his buyers might decide to go elsewhere for their merchandise. And that would make McAlistair haggle over the profits, which would mean less for Juan Quanta. Their little scene a few days earlier had left Quanta wary and seething, but he'd kill McAlistair before he'd let him cut the take.

He'd just wanted the boy. Young white males, strong and growing, like the *muchacho* in the yard with the cow, were worth *mucho dinero* south of the border. It had seemed like easy pickings, the lone woman, with no man about. The woman had been too old for selling and too full of fight for taming. She had to be killed before he could take the boy, of course. After all, she'd almost gotten him with the first salvo from that old shotgun. Then the boy had torn after him like a wildcat, clawing and biting like a lion cub when he, Quanta, had jerked the shotgun from the woman's hands and knocked her down on her back. The boy had been stronger than he'd expected, but a blow to his jaw had silenced him.

It was the woman who had surprised him with her strength. The kick to his groin had disabled him long enough for her to find a knife. Relishing the memory, he remembered how she'd tried to drive it into his back, only to fall with the weight of her blow as he'd rolled to one side. The fury in him had risen with an uncontrollable rage, giving him the strength that made him proud. When it had subsided, he felt spent and free, breathing deeply of the scent of his power of destruction.

It was a shame about the boy. He hadn't realized what he'd done, but the blow was fatal. Lost profit, especially the kind McAlistair didn't know about, always annoyed him. The Indians were a scruffy lot, but better pickings than usual. The women would bring more money than the children, who were too young for hard work in the fields.

Quanta thought of himself as a shrewd businessman. If there was a chance to make a peso or a dollar, he took it. The time would come when he would own his own show. Soon, he would be boss, the *padron* of a large *ranchero,* with many slaves working his land, his cattle. Slicking back his long, greasy hair, Juan Quanta took a quick look around at the horizon. Sometimes men tried to follow when he took the women, but this band was too decimated for heroics. He'd found this small settlement in the foothills, isolated and conveniently weak. Moving up from horses to humans had increased his self-esteem as well as his hoard of double eagles.

A child started wailing.

"Silence!" he snarled, wary of the noise. The mother tried to jostle the child into complying with the command, with no success. The whining grated on Quanta's nerves. He'd never liked moving children on the long ride; they were a burden and a nuisance.

Clicking back the hammer of his pistol, he cantered up beside the mother and child. "Now," he threatened, "the child stops this sniveling, or he dies."

The mother's eyes were slits, her feelings hidden. "Shh," she crooned. "You will not harm the child, or I will kill you." Her warning was quiet, but murder underlay every word.

"If I do not kill you and your rat, it will be because of the money I make off your stinking hides in Mexico, *comprende?* So do not push me far, or you will learn how little I can care for the price you bring." Quanta was suddenly tired of the whole lot of them, but it would do him no good to kill them all. Jerking his horse about, he loped to the rear of the small band. Maybe if he chewed one of the little peyote tablets now, he would feel better and forget about the stench and the hot, tiring ride to Mexico. Maybe.

Chapter Eight

THE ground was hard as Army biscuits. Hampered by his battered ribs, Moses tried using a pickax. Finally giving in to Wynoma's pleas for him to stop, he sat gasping with the pain and effort while she and Tyler chipped out a small grave. It took all three of them to carry Hope Hamill, wrapped in her Indian wool blanket, to the mound of broken earth.

"I wish I had time to find her a decent coffin. But she's been out too long as it is." Wynoma wiped the sweat from her face with her apron. " 'Sides, sooner she's under, the faster I can get this boy back to town. He'll stay around here like a stray dog if we don't start moving fast."

Wooden, the boy had helped Wynoma dig, the tears dried in pale paths on his dirty face. He hadn't said a word since his initial outburst.

Fetching a coffeepot from Mrs. Hamill's cookstove, Moses set it to boil on a small fire outside. None of them wanted to smell the powerful stench of old blood permeating the house.

"Tyler, describe the man who did this. Was he

tall, fat, thin, short, Indian, white? Can you tell me anything?"

Tyler's dark eyes suddenly flashed. "Half-Indian, half-Mex." Then it was as though he turned off the light and lapsed back into his melancholy. Moses looked to Wynoma for help.

"Anything else, Tyler? The more you can tell the marshal, the faster he can catch him. You want that, don't you?"

Tyler rocked, his arms locked about his knees. Kneeling beside him in the dirt, Wynoma encircled him with her arms. "Tell us, Tyler, please help."

Fetching a fistful of posters, Moses squatted beside the boy. "Take a look at these. Might be one of them."

At first Tyler stared into the distance as though he'd been struck blind. Moses held one, then another before the boy's eyes, hoping he'd see recognition in Tyler's expression. Tyler looked through each sheet of paper as though it weren't even there.

Wynoma took them and wrapped Tyler's fist about the bundle. "He'll look when he's ready, Marshal."

Turning to see to the horses, Moses felt his ribs scream once more. Stopping until the pain subsided, he felt the poster in his vest pocket. Quanta. Smoothing out the folds, he waited for a second.

"Got one more, Tyler. Think he's the one. Want to take a look?"

Tyler's gaze shifted to the marshal's face. "Any name?"

"Yes. Juan Quanta."

It was as though twenty years lifted off Tyler's shoulders. "He said that name, over and over. While he hit her. 'I am Quanta,' he shouted it, and he laughed. He *laughed!*" The tears fell again in torrents, while Wynoma cradled his head against her shoulder.

Moses stood by helplessly until the outburst was finished. "We'll have to stay the night. After you get these ribs bandaged, I should be able to ride. Tyler, did Mrs. Hamill have a horse?"

Staring at the marshal with vacant eyes, the boy nodded his head. Pointing to the shed, he looked away from Moses as though he wouldn't have known his own name even if it had been engraved on his hand in gold. Moses struggled to his feet as Wynoma leaned over to help him.

"Don't need help." He tried to shrug off her arm.

"Sure, like bees don't need honey. Don't be a fool," she hissed. "You're ailing, so don't act like it don't hurt." Following the marshal to the shed, she pulled back the double door. A sorry-looking bay swung his head to take a look at them.

"Not much of a horse," was Moses' only comment.

"She didn't need much. Just to get to town

once a month or so, to people when babies were due. Good thing Quanta didn't want him."

It was the first time they'd said the name to each other. "Didn't need him. Probably already had mounts for the Indians he plans to sell, and something this old won't bring a plugged nickel. Still, he could have taken the boy. I'm surprised he left him."

Wynoma's eyes darted to where the boy sat huddled by the fire in the growing twilight. "Must of figured he was dead. Or too much trouble for the effort. You sure it was Quanta? All kinds of men been drifting into the Territory since they started building the railroad. Not many of them good for much, just plain murderers and thieves. Most'll do anything to make a fast dollar."

"I don't see Mrs. Hamill as making any enemies, Wynoma. She was the sort to offer any man, good or bad, her hospitality. Besides, I believe the boy. He wasn't just grasping at any name." Moses tried to be gentle.

"Maybe not. But Miss Hope, she was white. Married a man with tribal rights and got to keep her land, legal-like. Most white folks resent that. All them that settled without any right, just squatting, maybe they set her up, had this done."

"Don't think so." Moses knew a slit throat wasn't the mark of a hired killer. Besides, Hope Hamill didn't have anything in the world worth stealing. The farm itself looked as if it could

On the Terror Trail 67

barely support her and the boy. "Soon as I can get this thing saddled in the morning, I'll head on out. Where'd you send the boy on my horse? I'll need her."

"That's just foolishness, and I won't hear another word of it!" Practically stamping her foot, Wynoma whirled to leave the shed. Chewing a mouthful of old hay, the bay swiveled to watch them. Reaching out, Moses pulled Wynoma to him.

"You and I know what's got to be done. Hope Hamill's just a small part of this, and we both know it. McAlistair's got to be stopped. If the tribes can't stop him, then the only law outside Fort Smith is me, and I'm not about to walk away from it."

"You've no idea what you're sticking your foot in, Marshal." Spitting the words, Wynoma shook off his restraining hand. "Things always been this way, and they aren't about to change just 'cause of you. What do you think one black man's going to do, up against the guns and men McAlistair's got?" Tears gathered in her eyes. "That's the way it's always been, some on top, some on the bottom. You know, after the war some tribes still refused to free their slaves? Well, now it's the Indians on the bottom of the pile. I'm sorry as I can be about Hope Hamill. She was one of my friends and I'd give my soul to bring her back from the dead, but you keep on, and you'll be as dead as she is."

As he pulled her gently toward him, Moses smelled the hot hay in the stall and the dusty coat of the bay. Wynoma was warm in his arms, like a coal burning from the center. "I spent most of my life doing what white folks wanted me to do—all the dirty work, anything and everything, including hunting down their own. This time, I got the law on my side. I'm going after Quanta, after McAlistair, and I aim to stop this slave running. I owe it."

"You don't owe nobody nothing!" Eyes ablaze, she pummeled his chest. "Why I'm bothering with the likes of you is beyond me. I should saddle up that horse, get him out of here so fast you'll have to walk out of the Territory." Slamming her palms into his ribs, she stopped in horror at what she'd done.

"Drat it, woman, that hurts. You're right—no call to bother with me. I take care of myself just fine." Stepping back, he encircled his aching sides with his arms. Wynoma stood before him, her hands suddenly weights at her thighs, her face wet with tears. Watching her sob quietly, he knew it was for Hope, for him, for all of them.

"Hush, that's enough now. Stop this carrying on—the boy needs you. You're all he's got." Stepping forward, he stroked her hair, crooning in a comforting voice. She stirred him too much—he'd known that from the first moment he'd seen her standing beside the big cookstove, her face surprised but trying to hide it as she

On the Terror Trail 69

looked from his face to the badge. Now all he wanted to do was take her in his arms, say the things a man says to a woman he wants to hold tight and feel warm and soft against his chest. It was the last thing he needed in his life. And the thing he wanted most at this moment.

Folding herself against him, Wynoma let the hurt and anger ebb out of her with the tears. She knew he was right, that the boy needed her more than anything else now. Besides, the marshal had made it clear he could, and wanted to, take care of himself, or so she repeated inwardly. Not at all sure it was a fact and not just a declaration, she looked up at him for reassurance, and she saw the softness and light in his eyes. Gently pressing herself to him, she knew she had her answer.

"If you've got to go, go. Don't leave me more to worry about than I've got now." Though her words were hard, her voice was sad.

"I'll be back once I've finished with McAlistair. Will you be all right?"

"Think I'll stay out here a spell with the boy, instead of taking him right back to town. Give things a while to cool down. No one'll know I'm gone for a while. They're used to me staying gone a week or so with a birthing. Vera'll keep the place open. Tyler's going to be the hard part. I'll have to say I found him wandering alone, dazed, and I don't know what happened to Hope." Running her hand along his broad back, she saw his eyes sparkle.

"Good idea. Keep that shotgun loaded, be ready to hide. Root cellar might work. Quanta just may decide to ride by on his way back from the border and check it out."

She tensed in his arms. "Never thought of that. It's a long haul from here to the border, traveling easy. We'll be gone by then. I'll hide Tyler with some friends."

He caressed her hair, soft and falling from the knot at the nape of her neck. Turning her face from his shoulder, she waited for a kiss. It was soft and kind, not what she'd expected.

He answered the question in her eyes. "Time for that later. I may be a while coming back, don't want you pining too hard for me, woman."

Laughing, she pulled him down to her lips once more. "Pine? I'll show you who's gonna pine!"

The question had been answered. "Okay, Marshal Moses, you go do what's gotta be done. Just make sure you come back alive. And those ribs better be all better, 'cause I intend on holding you real tight."

Grinning, he'd started to kiss her once more when they heard the boy screaming. Running ahead of him, Wynoma burst from the shed. "Tyler, what's wrong?"

"They always die, always!" Sobbing, the boy rocked back and forth on his heels at Hope's grave. "Every time I love someone, they get taken away from me. Same thing happened to my

On the Terror Trail 71

folks—men came riding by, shot them, took what they wanted from our wagon. Thought I was dead too, but I fooled them, just like I did that man who killed Hope, and now she's dead too. And I'm gonna make them pay, all them who done this!"

Wynoma tried to pull him off the grave. "Come on back to the fire, Tyler. Please."

Jerking free from her fingers, Tyler faced them both with his face twisted with grief and anger. "I'll kill him, I swear it."

In the space of seconds, the boy had aged to young manhood. Stepping back as the marshal moved toward him, he continued, "It's not your fight, Marshal, it's mine. I'll kill him, or die trying."

Wynoma gestured helplessly. "Nonsense, Tyler. You're just a boy. That's work for a man—a lawman. Come back to the fire, be a good boy now." Her voice trailed off helplessly. She'd seen the change, like a vision in church.

Moses watched the two of them late into the night, Wynoma staring at the boy like a mother about to lose her youngest to the gallows, feigning sleep every time he caught her eye. The boy pretended to doze, his arms twitching, fists clenching and unclenching, his jaw locked with the effort of trying to keep still. Moses knew the feeling and knew that it would drive the boy to action, right or wrong. Just before day, he saw both of them relax, and thought they'd finally drifted off into the sleep of total exhaustion.

As he saddled the bay quietly, his sides stung with the effort of lifting up the old saddle and tightening the cinch. But he knew it had to be that way, or the boy would find him, trail him into Mexico after Quanta. His chest tightened with the thought of not saying good-bye to Wynoma, but he closed that door behind him, locking it away with the memories of Jamie and all the good times. He had to find Quanta, and get to McAlistair through him. Only then would he be free to find Wynoma again.

He finally found Chloe in a small corral next to a tiny house on the outskirts of town. Waiting until dark, he'd approached the occupants, explaining who he was. Wide-eyed, they'd allowed him to take the mare, although they assured him that if he'd stolen that badge off the real marshal Miss Wynoma had told them to save the horse for, they'd come after him and see him hanged for a thief. Chuckling, he'd been impressed with their loyalty to Wynoma. Leaving the old bay behind, with instructions to keep him as hidden as possible, he'd headed for the border.

Cursing the loss of the day it had taken him to find Chloe, Moses dug his heels into the mare, stretching out her trot while he followed the well-used trail. Quanta would never stop for long if he expected someone to be following. While

Moses' instincts steered him on the long ride into Mexico, another part of him thought long and hard about the slaver and the man who controlled him.

The flat land swished beneath Chloe's hooves for days on end. Easing forward in the saddle, he hunkered down to let her find her own pace as the days rolled before him like blank tablets.

He'd seen so many men like McAlistair in years past, men who thought they owned the world and that it owed them every little thing and person they desired. It had galled him like wine gone bad to see the havoc they created in their whirlwinds of self-will, sucking up lives of ordinary people who asked nothing more of life than to be let alone. Petty tyrants usually had their own protection systems, sanctioned by the law and society, he mused. But this time he could do something about it. This time he was going to bring the pillars supporting McAlistair crashing down like the temple of the wicked. Quanta was going to be the first to fall.

He didn't really have a plan. In the past, his method had always been to see how the other side reacted to the threat he posed. Some folded, some fought, most were stunned at the sheer effrontery of being run to ground by a black man. How far Quanta would go to protect McAlistair was the big unknown.

He refused to accept Wynoma's analysis that in the final scheme of things there would always be someone on the bottom of the heap. Although his friendship with Jamie had started in boyhood, he had always been aware of the difference between them and that he had no control of his own destiny. The knowledge had been an unspoken barrier between them, one that admitted the one boy to the presence of the anointed, while leaving Leland Moses watching and waiting for the small tear in the temple veil that would give him the vision of the sanctum sanctorum, which would mean he was finally, eternally, everlastingly free. He would not, could not, permit the selling of anyone, white, black or red, man, woman or child, into involuntary servitude, even if it meant his life. No one deserved to be sold to the bottom of society, into the end of the world.

And what about Wynoma? Bedding down for the night in a small stand of cottonwoods, he propped his head on Chloe's saddle and chewed at the old rations from his saddlebags. He could still feel her hair in his hand, her kiss, her softness. If McAlistair refused to give up, would she have anything to come home to in the town owned and run by the white man? Knowing how hard she must have worked to build up her own business and to stay far enough out of McAlistair's way to avoid being a target, he had to admire her determination. And her ingenuity—he had to admit that he respected that. Women in his life had been mere transients. Nothing was wanted of them, nothing was expected. Did he know what he really wanted from Wynoma Webster?

"Chloe, what do you think?" As always, the sound of his words startled him when he'd passed some time without hearing the human voice.

Cocking her ears, Chloe looked up momentarily from her chomping. *Blast it!* he thought as he forced his hat brim down over his eyes and tried to fall asleep. *What I need now is an extra rifle and a steady shot, not some daydreams about a woman.*

The crackle of dried brush under hooves awoke him immediately. Lying still, he pretended to be asleep as the unshod intruder took a few more tentative steps. Chloe nickered gently to the visitor as Moses rolled to one side, his sidearm drawn and ready.

"Steady, or I'll shoot!" Shouting the warning, he prepared to fan the weapon at his enemy. Why he wasn't already dead was a puzzlement as he stared into the bore of a double-barreled shotgun not three feet from his face. In the darkness of the early dawn, he couldn't discern the features of his captor, seated on a large, swaybacked mule that kept trying to jerk the reins from its rider in order to reach for the grass Chloe had found so fascinating.

"So you've got me. What you gonna do now?" *Blast!* he cursed inwardly, unable to believe he'd been so foolish as to let himself be jumped.

"Nothing, Marshal. I intend on riding with you, that's all."

"I'll be danged! That you, Tyler?" Rolling to his feet, Moses reached into his vest pocket for a safety match. Nothing was darker than the moments before morning, and he didn't trust his ears. Striking the head on his boot, Moses cupped the flame in one hand and lifted it. It was Tyler all right.

"Get down off there, boy. Now!" Surprise and anger at having been bushwhacked by a mere boy made him harsher than he would normally have been with Tyler. "What on God's green earth got into you, running off and leaving Miss Wynoma all alone out at the Hamill place? How long you been dogging me? She know you're gone?"

"No, sir—well, maybe, I don't know, I 'spect she'll figure it out real soon now, when she notices her mule is gone and me with him. Been behind you most of the week. Anyway, this is something I've got to do by myself, and Miss Wynoma just wouldn't understand."

"You bet she wouldn't! Now get down here, boy, and tell me just what you think you're going to do." Moses already knew what Tyler was doing there. It went with the misery and anger that had held Tyler in its clutches since the death of Mrs. Hamill.

"I'm going to get him, Marshal. That man, the one who did it. And if you try to stop me, I'll shoot you too. I've spent my life, leastwise the part I lived with Mrs. Hamill, firing this old Betsy, and believe me, Marshal, I'm a pretty good shot by now." Spewing out the speech left Tyler breathless.

"Okay, Tyler, I believe you. So how about just stepping down off that poor excuse for an animal, and we'll talk about it. What do you say?" It had been a long time since Moses had been that age, and he searched his memory desperately for a way to talk to the boy without talking down to him. He knew that condescension would be a colossal mistake and that an unknown factor like Tyler could blow up the whole plan to get McAlistair like jars of nitro.

"All right, but just you mind, I'm coming with you or going on without you. But I'm going after the man who killed Miss Hope."

Watching the boy dismount, Moses noticed that the shotgun was always ready. Wary, that was how Tyler was feeling, so it was up to Moses to make him trust him, at least enough to go home and forget about Quanta.

"Come on over to the fire. I'll stir up these coals and see if we can't get some water warm. Got a few grounds of coffee left, want some?" Man talk was the only way to get the boy to listen.

"Sure, been riding hard to catch up with you. Why'd you double back to town?"

Moses watched the boy squat beside him at the fire, the shotgun resting on his knees, one finger still on a trigger for one barrel. "Needed my horse. Wasn't going far on Mrs. Hamill's. So you didn't tell Miss Wynoma what you were doing, just went off and stole one of her mules?"

Bristling, Tyler stopped chewing the jerky Moses had given him. "Didn't steal it. Just borrowed it, since I knew we'd pick her up on the way back to Fort Smith with that buzzard. If'n I don't kill him first."

"Tyler, I understand how you feel. A man has to take a price back from those who've taken what's dear to him. But that's not always the best frame of mind, tends to make a man hotheaded, careless when he should be watching. I know—I've seen a lot of it in my business."

Tyler's pale eyes shone in the small flicker of the fire. "No use trying to talk me out of it, Marshal. You let me ride with you, or I go it alone. Don't make me no difference, but I'm going to get the man who killed Miss Hope." Chewing slowly, he turned his face away.

"Drat it all, Tyler! Don't be so all-fired stubborn. Or maybe I should say 'stupid.' I can't take you with me—you might get hurt, be in the way when I need a clear shot." Forgetting his tack, Moses sputtered with frustration at the boy's stiff-necked single-mindedness.

"I can take care of myself, Mr. Marshal. This here's a free country, and I can go where I please." The finality in the boy's words startled

On the Terror Trail

Moses. There was to be no arguing with him, he'd decided.

"All right, I'll make a deal with you, then. You stay out of my way, do what I tell you, when I tell you, and no arguing, you hear? I say jump, you jump, and fast. Otherwise, I may as well shoot you now, get it over with."

A faint smile crossed the boy's lips, whether at the ultimatum or at the fact that he'd won a partial victory, Moses didn't know.

"Sure, if you say so. So when do we ride?"

Moses knew Tyler had pushed hard and long to find him. Still, there was no time to waste. He'd have to think of a way to handle the boy before the showdown with Quanta. Maybe if he wore him out enough, he could leave him on the trail and pick him up on the way back.

"Now. Douse the fire. I'll saddle Chloe."

Blast it! he cursed as he once more struggled with the saddle and his broken ribs. Before he could choke back a groan, the boy was beside him, reaching for the cinch straps.

"You never did let Wynoma tape them ribs, did you?"

"Don't need it. They'll mend just fine." Stepping back, he let the boy finish the saddling. They mounted and rode off together, the silence between them like a heavy sky laden with the makings for a tornado.

The last thing on earth Leland Moses needed was to nursemaid a boy bent on revenge. Yet he understood how Tyler felt, and that made it all the worse.

The land stretched before them like taffy. Treeless for miles and miles, it ate their patience and tempers. Moses wiped his hands on his pants, feeling the heat burning the soles of his feet. They'd been on the trail to Mexico for weeks.

"Want to stop early? Rest up some?"

Tyler shook his head. "Gotta keep moving. We should find him sometime soon, right?"

Moses suppressed a groan. "Don't you think of anything else, boy? I swear, you're the most one-tracked individual I've ever met." Tyler had grated on him with his consistency.

"Nope. How far to Mexico now?"

"Far as it was about an hour ago when you asked."

They were closer than he wanted Tyler to know. The moment of decision wasn't far off, and he hadn't decided how to handle Tyler. The last thing he needed was to have the simmering fury of the boy erupt when he least needed the distraction.

The horses were tired, their shoes worn. "Well, I intend on resting here a spell. The Rio Grande's not far, and I expect we'll find something on the other side of the border."

He knew Tyler understood what he meant. They dismounted together, dropping reins where

On the Terror Trail 81

the horses stood. Moses offered Tyler a swig from his canteen. The mule nibbled at Chloe's mane.

Tyler stretched out on the hard, sun-baked ground. "My bottom's about had it. I've never seen the Rio Grande."

"Not much to see. We'll cross just after sundown. Don't want any advertisement that we're coming."

Propped on his elbows, Tyler cocked his head. "You done this afore?"

Moses wiped his face with his bandanna. "Some. Best to keep low. Gringos aren't too well liked in most border towns, especially wearing a star."

"So I'll go in alone, find out what we need to know." Tyler's voice was eager.

Snorting, Moses lifted Chloe's hoof to check the throat. "Think again, friend. You ready?"

Tyler rolled to his feet. "You're the one who wanted to stop." His tone was sulky.

"So ride." Moses was peeved at his own snappishness. It wasn't going to be easy to let Tyler down.

The river, when they finally reached it, curled before them, a pale silver ribbon beneath a cloudless sky. The last of the sun cut red swaths across the deep teal of early nightfall.

"We're here. I want you to stay on this side. It's too dangerous now for you." Moses kept his voice low, expecting an outburst.

Tyler was silent for a few moments, stroking

the stiff hair of the mule's mane. "You got it wrong, Marshal. I'm still coming with you, like it or not. If'n you decide to shake me somehow, I'll catch up." There was a finality to his words that made Moses believe him.

Spurring Chloe down the soft bank into the shallows, Moses didn't look back. He'd seen the cut in the other side, and aimed Chloe deeper into the pull of the Rio Grande. Pulling at the reins, Chloe took the bit and waded through. Moses pushed on to the other bank, into Mexico, knowing the town he wanted wasn't far and that Tyler would follow, no matter what.

It was nothing more than a few shacks and a cantina on the way to nowhere. Moses saw the lone light of the cantina and pulled up. Looking back, he saw the boy dogging him. Tyler was on the ragged edge of exhaustion, the skin around the edges of his lips white with the effort of keeping up. Still, he'd hung to Chloe's trail, his back hunched with fatigue, the mule plugging along at a bone-cracking trot. Moses wondered how long he'd last. It would be a lot easier to drop him off somewhere, pick him up after he himself had taken care of Quanta.

"Hey, boy, swing your legs on down here. Thought we'd stop a spell." Tying Chloe to the hitching rack, he looked into Tyler's tight, dirty face.

The boy stared back, his hands clutching the

rope reins of the mule. "No time for that. We gotta keep moving. He'll be into Mexico soon."

"I know that." Moses tried to keep the annoyance out of his voice. "But Chloe here's plumb worn out, and I could use a plate of hot beans and rice myself. If you aren't all that tuckered out—well, why don't you just sit here. I'll be with you in a while." He was beginning to regret his earlier harshness.

"Well, if that's the way it's gonna be. . . ." Mumbling under his breath, Tyler slid off the mule.

Hiding his grin, Moses eased aside the doors of the cantina, his gun hand free. At least it would give them both some time out of the constant heat and give him a chance to figure out what he was going to do with the boy. Quanta was close, he knew it from the trail. If he pushed much more, he'd end up riding on top of the outlaw, and the boy would get in the way for sure. A dog howled in the distance, and Moses was instantly alert. *Blast!* he thought. *I should have put the badge away.*

The dirty barkeep watched them with wary eyes. Swirls of dust followed the Anglos through the swinging door, the paint cracked and bitten with sun and age.

"What do you want to eat, Tyler?" Throwing his hat on the table, Moses placed the back of the hand-hewn chair against a wall. The boy stared.

"Whatever you're having, Marshal. You know

as well as me that we're almost on top of him. We oughta keep moving. Why're you stopping now?" His hands were white as he clutched the edge of the table.

He ignored Tyler's question. "Señor, *frijoles,* some beer. Plenty of both." He watched the barkeep's hands as they slid beneath the chewed counter.

Pulling two mugs of beer, the Mexican eased his way to their table. "Señor, you wear the star. A ranger? Seeking Indians who kill and steal?" The oily voice slid its way into Moses' bad humor.

"No, señor. *Federale.* Marshal. I seek a *pistolero.*" It was dangerous, letting on in this rattlesnake pit of a village that he was hunting Quanta. The slave-runner probably met his buyers here.

"Then you come for business or pleasure?" The Mexican's black teeth showed in an insincere smile.

"Food, señor. As you can see, the *muchacho* is hungry, and we have come far."

"Ah, yes, they all do." With a knowing wink, the Mexican turned to shout their orders to the back of the hovel.

Dismissing the man's innuendoes, Moses decided the truth was the only way out. Tyler probably could handle it better than most his age. "You're right. We could be on top of them by tomorrow, the next day maybe, if we kept at it. But, Tyler, well—" He paused. "No easy way to say it, but I'm going to leave you here. Pick you up on the way back. I need to be free to move fast, and you're just going to get in the way."

Moses gestured for another bottle of the local beer for both of them. "Tyler, I respect how you feel, but you've got to let me do my job, my way."

Picking at his worn nails, Tyler fought for control. "You can't make me stay behind. I'll follow you, even ride on ahead." Defiance edged Tyler's voice, as though he knew he was about to lose this one, but he'd go down fighting.

"Not if I were to ask you to stay here, you wouldn't. I'd trust your word of honor. Otherwise, I just might have to tie you up hog-style, leave you at the hitching post." Moses took a swig of the warm beer and watched Tyler's face.

Holding the bottle between his clenched fists, Tyler kept a cork on his own anger. "No need for that, Marshal. But you're likely to need a back-up man, someone to help you."

"Not this time, Tyler. Maybe another day, but I think I can handle this one alone. Not that I wouldn't be honored to have you back me up, but, well, this one's a little tricky, and I feel like one man alone's going to have a better chance." He admired the boy's guts and the courage and pride that were making him into a man before his eyes.

"Then how long do I wait for you here?" Tyler glanced around the barren, whitewashed walls of the cantina, his face forlorn.

"Just a few days at the most. I'll make arrangements for you to stay somewhere, pick you up on the way back to McAlistair."

"McAlistair! You're not taking the buzzard back there, are you?" Sputtering his beer, Tyler jerked to his feet.

"Got to. Need to take McAlistair in too. Might as well do it all in one trip. Fort Smith's too far to go doing it more than once."

Slamming his open palms on the rough planks of the table, Tyler choked on anger. "Then you're dead, Marshal, and you just don't know it yet. Even I know you aren't going to get them into Fort Smith alone." Tyler was speaking with an authority beyond his years.

"Then I want you to promise me you'll take care of Miss Wynoma, make sure nothing bad happens to her. Can you promise me that, Tyler?"

Sinking into his seat, Tyler dropped his hands back to his lap. "Yes, sir. Least I can do, I reckon. Miss Hope would've made me promise the same."

"Good. If McAlistair's men find out she helped me, she might need a man's help."

The boy bristled with pride at Moses' designation of his status. "You're going to need a man to ride with you too, Marshal, so you just let me know when."

"I'll do that, Tyler. Believe me, you're first on my list."

On the Terror Trail

The mangy barkeep threw plates before them. He'd listened to every word he could hear, and he wondered why the man bothered with the whining boy.

Wolfing down the spicy food, each was lost in plans for the future. Finally finished, Moses pushed back his plate and called for the owner of the cantina.

"Señor, I wonder if I could make arrangements for this young man to stay in your lovely town until I return?" The sarcasm wasn't lost on the barkeep. "I'll be back for him soon, and I want him to enjoy a clean bed while I am gone."

The plump Mexican gazed in puzzlement from the black man to the thin, gangling boy. "I suppose so, if the price is right. You are not taking him to the market?"

His hackles up, Moses returned the man's puzzlement with a cold, hard stare. "See this?" Thrusting his arm under the man's nose, he reached with the other for the star. "I'm a Federal Marshal, señor, not a slaver. I don't buy and sell people. I've been bought and sold myself." He struggled to regain his temper. "This young man is my"—he thought for a moment—"deputy. Treat him with the respect due the representatives of the law of this country."

The barkeep raised one bushy eyebrow, his contempt barely concealed. "He'll bring much *dinero*. Strong, young boy like that, you are a fool, gringo."

"You make sure he's here when I get back, eh, señor? Because, if he isn't, I'll hold you responsible. And that could be very unpleasant." The dog howled once again in the darkness. Moses stared into the Mexican's blank eyes. "*Comprende, señor?*"

"*Sí.*" Twirling on his heel, the man retreated to his bar.

Standing, Moses held out his hand for Tyler's. Shyly, Tyler wiped his palm on his pants, then returned the grip. The large black fist enveloped the thinner white one. "Be ready to ride whenever I get back, okay, Deputy?" Moses winked at Tyler and was surprised to see a soft smile on the boy's face.

"Sure enough, Marshal. Whenever you say."

Moses fished in his saddlebags. "Miss Hope teach you to read?"

Puzzled, Tyler nodded. "The Good Book. Read it every morning before breakfast."

"Then here's something to keep you occupied until I get back." Handing the chamois-wrapped Keats to Tyler, Moses watched the boy unwrap the book.

"Be careful. It's right old."

As he felt the worn leather edges of the binding, Tyler's face shone. Moses knew he understood the importance of the volume.

"I will."

Moses mounted and pushed Chloe out at a slow trot. But he paused on the edge of the village, just to make sure Tyler was standing at the dilapidated cantina. To his amazement, the boy waved. Returning the gesture with one quick sweep of his arm, he put his heels to Chloe's sides. It had been easier than he'd expected to talk the boy into staying. But already he missed him. It was lonely once again. *Watch out for the chiggers and the bedbugs, little one,* he thought, seeing Tyler's empty, disappointed face before him as he pushed deeper into Mexico.

Chapter Nine

It was a toss-up. Considering his options, Moses knew it would be wiser to wait for Quanta to return from his foray into whatever slave market he used in Mexico than to try to stop him from getting there. But letting Quanta sell the Indians stuck in his craw more than he could live with. He knew he would have to catch him now, before Quanta made his sale.

Quanta was making no effort to conceal his trail in Mexico. Evidently he'd decided he had a fast path into the border towns specializing in the selling of human flesh, and he didn't bother to take any of the precautions Moses assumed he knew. Feeling it would be wiser to push ahead and cut him off, Moses cursed his own pride that demanded he take both the bait and the big fish. Tyler had been right; it would have been better to have a back-up man. But he had to go it alone, and he intended to do it as quickly as possible. That meant he'd see Tyler, and Wynoma, all the sooner.

The rutted wagon path he followed into the next wide-open border town cut through land barren and burned. The frightened villagers he encountered answered his questions with flicks of the eyelid, with stares in the direction he was heading. The poverty he saw reminded him of blacks in the South after the war, barely working a living from stone-and-stump-filled land. He stopped asking at the dusty adobe shanties when he found the sign of at least ten horses, tired and on their last legs. It had been too many days. Chloe picked up her pace when he asked it of her, but he felt her strain.

Cutting around the path he'd found, he decided to make his stand. It was night when he chose his spot, a rocky point that gave him the best view of his surroundings. Pulling his hat low over his eyes, he willed his muscles to relax. The handful of dried beans he'd bought from a round-faced silent woman in one of the hovels rested on his belly like bullets. He wanted this to be over with, finished, his job done, so he could get back to Wynoma. The ache within him to end the tension was like nothing he'd felt before, and with amazement he realized it was because he cared for someone, something, other than himself.

He awoke late the next morning, the sun already high in the sky. Unkinking his back, he swigged from the canteen, then fed Chloe what was left of the grain.

After checking his rifle, he chose a small stand of mesquite as his vantage point. He tied Chloe to a few twigs, knowing she'd sleep with one hind foot cocked until he needed her. There was no real cover, but it would have to do. With any luck at all, he'd get some help from the Indians, if they weren't already beaten into the ground.

Squatting, he rested the rifle on his knees and listened for the sounds he knew would come. Some people scouted by smell, some by sign alone, but he'd always trusted his sense of hearing more than any other. It was at times like this that he wondered what he was doing out here, likely to get shot by a man who didn't deserve the time of day, much less to live. But at this moment it worried him more than most. And he knew why. It was Wynoma's doing, her and the boy's. They'd managed to mean more to him in a few short days than he'd ever intended, ever wanted. For the first time in ages, he cared about surviving. And that wasn't a good feeling for a Federal Marshal to have, because it made for caution when daring was what was needed most.

Pulling a short drink from his canteen, he felt he wouldn't have too long to wait. Just as he was about to check his rifle for the umpteenth time, he heard it.

At first it was a minor vibration, like unshod hooves on hard ground; then it grew to the faint swish and creak of saddle leather, bits, tails fighting flies. Flattening himself to the ground, he took aim in the direction of the sound.

The first riders in his sights hung on horseback like shadows of what had once been proud people. Women and small children drooped, their heads down with fatigue and loss of hope. Quickly using his spyglass, Moses picked out Quanta at the back of the pack, his dark face dreamy, his sway in the saddle unsteady at best. Looking at the slashes in the clothing of the women, Moses knew that Quanta had beaten his captives into submission long before this moment. Quanta swayed softly in the saddle, his head nodding. Obviously the gunman was in no condition to do much fighting. Moses wondered if it was fatigue or something else that had made the slaver so careless.

Suppressing a small grunt of satisfaction, Moses stood, rifle at his shoulder. "Drop your weapons, Quanta. This is the law, and you're under arrest." His words awoke the captives, but Quanta still smiled abstractly at the horizon.

"Hear me, Quanta? Drop them now, or I shoot!" Moses meant it. No matter what happened next, he would kill Quanta if he didn't obey.

The Indians remained in stony silence, their eyes darting from Moses to Quanta and back again. Then, all at once, a woman with a child in her arms dropped from the pony she rode and tried to run for Moses.

"Get down!" he barked. Just as he had feared, Quanta pulled a Colt with a swiftness his lackadaisical pose belied and fired. Falling to the ground in silence, the woman was still.

"All right, you asked for it," Moses snarled. Pulling the trigger with deliberate aim, he blasted the *pistolero*'s gun out of his hand. The devil would never hold a gun in his right hand again, he thought with grim satisfaction.

Yelping with pain, Quanta grabbed his wounded hand as though holding a hot coal. "Why you, you—" Quanta's epithet was drowned out by a shout of anger and relief from the Indians. Almost in unison, they swarmed from their horses and reached with vengeful hands to haul the slaver into the dirt. Struggling to escape from the pummeling of their fists, Quanta rolled away, toward Moses, blood from his hand staining the dirt.

Stepping out from the mesquite, Moses jammed the rifle against Quanta's head. Pushed aside, the Indians reluctantly stood back and let Moses take toll of the damage to the slave runner.

"You're lucky I don't let them kill you, Quanta. But it's worth more to me to see McAlistair's face when I bring you back to town in handcuffs, primed and ready for the Federal prison. And if you aren't real nice to me on the way back to McAlistair, you won't have any need for handcuffs, that's for sure, 'cause you'll be hog-tied on that fancy Spanish saddle of yours. And don't count on being alive at the same time."

Quanta's glazed eyes tried to focus on Moses' face. "What's the matter, you want a piece of the profits? No problem, we'll talk. . . ." His slurred speech drifted off as Moses jerked him upright and tied a quick tourniquet about the bleeding hand.

"Don't make that mistake again, Quanta. I'm a Federal Marshal, and you're going in for horse thievin', killing, slave running, and anything else I can come up with before we get to a telegraph. And I get right upset with scum like you who think I'm ripe for bribery. Makes me want to do things, like shoot off other parts of their bodies." Grinning widely, Moses stared into Quanta's beady black eyes, the thin eyebrows making him look surprised at such an outpouring of outrage. But Moses knew his brain was beginning to function, and the situation was sinking in at last.

"Sure as shooting, McAlistair's going to be glad to see you, and having you in one piece might make identification easier, far as the price offered by the United States for your worthless hide is concerned." Turning to the Indians, Moses tried to smile. But the hate and desperation in their eyes stopped him from any attempts at levity.

"You folks, you speak English? Can you get back to your homes alone?" He hadn't counted on having to nursemaid the group back to their reservation lands.

A tall, thin woman, older than the rest, spoke up. "We can get there. Just leave us some water, if you can. The children are thirsty."

"Hate to do this—leave you, I mean." Tossing

his canteen to her, Moses saw for the first time that this was a pacified group of one of the bigger tribes.

"We'll make it—if we don't run into more slavers." Her voice was bitter. "What about him, Marshal? You really going to take him back to McAlistair? Then you're a bigger fool than you know. In case you didn't hear, Quanta works for McAlistair." Her educated English cut into him with its hatred.

"Yes, ma'am, I know." Tying Quanta's hands to the pommel, he avoided her eyes. He knew she was thinking he planned to cut himself into McAlistair's little empire, show the boss man that a black could do a better job as a slaver than the man currently on the payroll.

"Where can I find you and your people if it's necessary for trial?" He didn't feel like answering her unspoken questions.

"Up in the Pottawatomie lands." Gesturing to the others, she sent them scurrying back to their mounts. Suddenly, his sixth sense told him someone was approaching at a dead run.

"Get out of the way!" he barked, pulling his six-shooter. He hadn't planned on this, and the thought of being trailed himself by some of McAlistair's men ran down his back like the cold hand of death.

Holding the pistol to Quanta's head, he snarled into his ear, "You make one wrong move, and your brains are going to be splattered all over this

On the Terror Trail 97

godforsaken border." Pulling back the action, he waited for the rider to appear.

His farsightedness had served him in good stead in his line of work. But this time he couldn't believe his eyes: the mule doing a steady lope, the boy on its back riding with the ancient shotgun resting across its withers.

"Blast it all!" Moses spit out, cursing his luck in ever meeting Hope Hamill and her foster son, Tyler.

Seeing the group in the distance, Tyler stood in the wooden stirrups, balancing the shotgun against his hip as he pushed the mule into a faster lope. "Need help, Marshal?"

His voice cracked on the words. Reining in about five feet from the horse bearing Quanta, Tyler avoided looking Moses in the eyes. "Thought you might need me, that's all."

In icy silence, Moses put his foot in Chloe's stirrup and swung up. "You people are free to ride with us as long as you want. Get mounted."

"But, Marshal, this old shotgun might have done the trick for you, you never know. . . ." Pleading, the boy tried to get Moses to take notice of him.

"Not now, Tyler." Moses spit out the words. Stupid fool boy, if there'd really been trouble, he would probably have been killed, and Moses could never have explained it satisfactorily to Wynoma.

"But, Marshal. . . ." Tyler reached out to touch

Chloe. "If you'll hold up a second, I can explain."

"No explaining, Tyler. You lied to me. No way around it."

"Well, not exactly. I did stay there, at that cantina, for a while. I never promised I wouldn't follow you."

Moses leveled his hard eyes on the boy. "Don't be technical with me, boy. I know all about technicalities, and it all boils down to the same thing. I trusted you and you couldn't be trusted."

Quanta had pulled himself out of his drug-induced stupor enough to catch the drift of the chastisement. "You think you're going to get me back to stand trial, you dog? You can't even keep a wet-nosed boy out of your way!" Cackling wildly, Quanta jerked suddenly to one side, driving his Spanish spurs into the sides of his horse. Screaming with pain, the bay shied to the right, knocking Chloe into a quick twirl. Caught off balance, Moses reached for the bay's one dangling rein, and found himself being dragged from the saddle by the bay's bolt from the spurs.

A shotgun blast cut into the air just as Moses was about to fall to the ground. Quanta twisted in the saddle, slumping forward as blood spurted from his shoulder and ear.

"Tyler, grab Chloe!" Stumbling to his feet, Moses dragged the terrified bay to a halt, pulling Quanta from the saddle.

"You pig!" Moses threw the outlaw in the dirt

as Quanta writhed with pain from where the shotgun pellets had caught him. "Try anything like that again, and I'll kill you myself." Cursing himself inwardly for being such a fool as to let Quanta get that far, he chanced a quick look at Tyler. The boy stared at the outlaw with an adult satisfaction written all over his face, as though he'd finally scratched an itch that had been eating at him for too long.

"Thanks, Tyler," he mumbled as he checked the superficial damage to Quanta's shoulder.

"Any time, Marshal. Told you I'd make a good back-up man." Tyler cracked the shotgun and reloaded.

"Maybe, but only when I tell you I want one, you hear me? From now on out, you do as I say, or I'll fill your backside so full of buckshot you won't sit down again for a month of Sundays." He was getting careless, and the knowledge made him lash out at Tyler more than he knew he should.

He couldn't tell if Tyler had been properly chastened or if it was just a good act. Once more lashing Quanta, bandaged and more bloodied, to the pommel, Moses wrapped the bay's reins about his own pommel. Turning in the saddle, he surveyed the motley band of Indians and the white boy on the mule, all gathered behind him like the lost tribes of Israel.

Lord, give me strength, he prayed as he pushed

Chloe back in the direction they'd traveled just that morning. "Tyler, keep a lookout, you hear?"

He could hear the pride in the boy's answer. "Yessir, Marshal, anything you say."

Nothing so far had gone as he'd planned it. Moses wondered how long it would be before the next surprise.

They stopped briefly at the small border town they'd first entered, to allow the Indians to rest up. Using some of his own money, Moses bought them canteens and rations, along with a hot meal at the same cantina. The women had recuperated more quickly than he'd expected, as though hope and freedom were the tonic they'd needed.

"I can take you across the river, get you started through Texas." He spoke to the gathered group, their tattered garments and skeletal wrists reminding him of the first recruits he'd seen in the Army transport going to Fort Leavenworth so many years before.

"We can make it from here, Marshal." One of the women stepped forward, taking both his hands in hers. Her seamed face smiled up at him. "We know the way home."

He watched them go, feeling as though he'd abandoned a charge, given up something entrusted to him too cheaply. Handcuffing Quanta to the horse railing, he decided to take time himself for another meal at the cantina.

When Moses appeared once more in the door

On the Terror Trail   101

of his place, the eyes of the proprietor came alight with greedy anticipation. "You return, Señor Federale Marshal? It is clear to see you have your prize and the slaves also. How clever you are—two prizes for one effort. Now you will collect for the slaver and get the price of the slaves also!" He practically rubbed his hands together with glee at the thought of all the money the marshal would have to spend on watered-down liquor that night in the cantina. He was willing to take credit, knowing that the marshal would wait in town for the telegraph that would assure his bounty to be sent.

Something inside Moses cracked, and all the venom came pouring out like oil on fire.

"Don't you ever call a United States Marshal a slave trader, or you're going to find yourself dead, and it won't be from your own cooking." Jerking the owner to him, he thrust his dark-skinned forearm in the man's face. "What color is that? How often do I have to tell you, you idiot, that I don't buy and sell flesh. No one who's been sold— Oh, why do I bother? Are you blind, deaf, and dumb?" He knew it was hopeless to get the man to understand.

The barkeep pulled back, his eyes wide with surprise. "No, señor, I am not blind. But what would you have me do? I am as willing as the next man to make a profit. Why shouldn't you?"

Turning away in disgust, Moses stopped dead in his tracks. Framed by the intense sun, Tyler stood in the doorway of the cantina. "That true, Marshal? Did you plan on making money off those Indians?"

Snorting with anger, Moses pushed past the boy. "Don't be a fool, Tyler. Once a man's been a slave himself, he's not about to do the same to anyone else." He calmed himself down, realizing it did no good to vent his frustrations on the boy. "Let's go find ourselves some tins of peaches, have a little party before we hit the trail. What do you say, Deputy?"

Pulling a can from his saddlebag, Moses punched the top with his knife. Tyler watched in fascination as the thick sweet syrup began to bubble up from the cut.

"Why'd anybody do that, Marshal—own someone else, I mean?" Fishing out a peach with his fingers, Tyler sucked on it whole.

"All kinds of reasons, none of them good. I got told when I was a boy that bondage was part of the Bible, and God just meant for some folks to be owned, some to be owners. Way I see it, Jesus set us all free." He was surprised at his own response to the boy. But he must have said the right thing, because Tyler didn't ask any more questions.

"Reckon you're right. Miss Hope read me right much from the Bible, teaching me to read and all. Figure she'd agree with you." It was a good sign, Moses thought, that Tyler was letting go of some of the grief and anger, that he could talk about Mrs. Hamill without withdrawing into revenge.

Wiping his fingers on his pants, the boy shook his head. "Still think we're crazy to head for McAlistair. That's going to be nothing but trouble, Marshal. Most folks there figure they're the sort who are the owners, and they own the rest of the world, you and me included. Don't know how you're going to convince them otherwise."

His humor restored by Tyler's matter-of-factness, Moses cleaned the knife blade in the horse trough, carefully wiping it dry with the bandanna he'd untied from his neck.

"Don't need convincing, Tyler. We—" He stopped in his tracks. What was he doing, including Tyler in his harebrained scheme? "I," he corrected, "just have to get them into Fort Smith, that's all."

Tugging at the mule's fetlock, Tyler cradled one big hoof between his knees. Checking it for any lodged stones, he hid his face from Moses. "Well, then, I reckon we'd better get going. Soon as we get this job done, I can get back to milking the cow."

Moses let it ride. There was too much to explain for the moment, and he didn't intend on shattering the boy just when he seemed more like himself, full of spunk like the first time he'd seen him at the Hamill ranch.

"Get up, Quanta." Moses unlocked the handcuffs, jerking the slaver to his feet. "You feeling a mite poorly about now? Well, just to show you how nice I can be, have some." Pushing his canteen into the man's manacled hands, he watched him gulp down the water. "You didn't do that much for those Indians, did you, Quanta? But then again, you didn't have to guarantee what kind of shape they were in once you got them to market, did you? Well"—he paused, retying the canteen to his saddle—"I don't make guarantees, either."

The menace in the words wasn't lost on Quanta. For the first time since the effects of the peyote had worn off, he spoke. "You'll never make it."

"Oh, yes, I will. Now get up in that saddle. We got some riding to do."

The slaver's thick, hateful laughter echoed behind them as they rode out of town. Moses knew his plan had better be good, or Quanta's prediction would come all too true.

Chapter Ten

*L*ORD *forgive me,* Wynoma thought, *but I'm about to turn into a cursing woman.* The disappearance of both Tyler and the mule could mean only trouble, and she just didn't feel like handling anything else at the moment. Images of Hope Hamill kept her awake enough, and it didn't do her any good to add worry about Tyler to the anxiety she felt for the marshal.

She should just have served him that piece of apple pie and sent him on his way. That was how she'd managed so far to stay out of trouble in McAlistair, by minding her own business and not asking too many of the wrong sort of questions. But this time something had happened, and even though she wasn't young or foolish enough to believe in love at first sight, she had to admit she'd been mighty taken with the man. Part of her hoped she'd never see him again, that he'd forget all about McAlistair and keep on riding, but the selfish part wished just the opposite with all her heart. It had been a while since this sort of foolishness had hit her this hard, and she was still a little angry that she'd let it.

Yet Tyler was part of the worry also, and he had nothing to do with Leland Moses. At least, he hadn't originally. Sure as shooting, though, Tyler had lit out after the marshal and was planning on taking some hand in the business with the gunfighter and McAlistair. His misery had been an open wound that only revenge could heal, but she hadn't had a chance to tell him that it would be the kind of scar that would fester within until he gave up the hatred. He was her responsibility now, just as if Hope had put the boy's hand in hers, and she had to do all she could to keep him out of McAlistair's destructive path.

Harnessing the sole mule left to her claptrap wagon, she thought carefully about her next step as she buckled each strap.

"Well, Beulah, what do you think? Do I play this like poker, hide my weak points, do some big bluffing, or fold up and head on home?" Rubbing the mule between the ears, she thought suddenly of her café, her business. It was time she got back. Vera would be anxious, and heaven knew how many customers she'd have poisoned with her cooking.

Climbing up, she allowed herself one last glimpse of Hope's small grave. "It'll work out right, my friend," she promised the mound of dirt. "I'll take care of Tyler somehow."

Wynoma snapped the reins on Beulah's dusty hide, and the wagon lurched out of the home-

On the Terror Trail

stead. She knew what she had to do next, and it was time she moved out.

A few hours later, she hitched the mule to the front porch of the small ranch house. "Hello there, it's me, Wynoma." She searched the horizon for signs of the man of the place. A puff of dust in the distance assured her that he wasn't going to be underfoot.

A very pregnant young Indian woman waddled to the door, opening it wide for the midwife. "Lordy, Wynoma, you gave me a start! I've been canning pole beans. Come on in. Aren't you a little early?"

Wynoma wiped her hot and dusty face. "How you can be putting up beans in this heat is beyond me, Emma. You should be sitting in a rocker here on the porch, taking it easy, not standing over a hot cookstove!"

Laughing, Emma took Wynoma by the hand and pulled her into the small, one-room house. "You know me, Wynoma—the busier I am about now, the happier I'll be when the baby gets here. But it's another month, at least, or didn't I tell you that?"

"You told me." Wynoma untied her broad-brimmed sun hat and swept a cat off a handmade chair beside the cookstove. "Now, you have a seat. I'll do the stirring for a while, 'cause I'll be needing a favor from you, Emma."

Lowering herself laboriously into the chair, the woman wiped her shining face with her feed-sack apron. "Does feel good to sit a spell, I'll give you that. So what's the favor?"

"Firstwise, I have to ask you to keep this from your husband. He's a good man, and I don't want to see him get caught in any of McAlistair's traps, so it's better if we keep this between us. I need for you to say, if anyone asks, that I came out here to stay with you a few days, just in case. After all, the last one was a few weeks early."

"You in some kind of trouble, Wynoma?" Emma's smooth, brown face became wrinkled with concern.

"No, Emma, not me. But Hope Hamill's dead, been killed."

Emma stared as though Wynoma's mouth had misspoken and she'd just heard the wrong words.

"Killed? You mean, she's dead? We must tell Harry. He'll get to town, bring back the sheriff, a posse. . . ." Her voice trailed off as Wynoma shook her head.

"This wasn't the work of any marauders, or the like. It's the doing of one of McAlistair's men. Not pretty, and the boy, Tyler, lived to tell us what happened—at least, what he could. That's where I need your help. I took the Federal Marshal out there, to heal up from a beating he took at McAlistair's orders. Found Miss Hope dead. And now the marshal's lit off after the man who did it, and seems like Tyler's followed him."

She paused and gave the beans a vicious stir. "The way I see it, that marshal isn't about to quit

On the Terror Trail

until he pulls in the man who did the killing, and McAlistair with him. That is, if he lives long enough. And if he don't, I'll still have to find a way to keep Tyler out of McAlistair's way. But if the marshal gets back to town and does what I think he's planning on doing, I've got to be around to help him out. That's the least I can do, seeing as Hope Hamill was one of the kindest, most Christian women I've ever known."

Emma fanned herself with her apron. "What do you need for me to do, then?"

"If anyone should ask, tell them I've been here. I'm heading back for town now, and far as I'm concerned, I don't even know Hope's dead—I haven't seen her in a month or more. I came out here to check on you, we did a little canning, and I expect to be back in a few more weeks. Now you see why I want to keep your man out of this. He'll feel like he has to go barging on out of here and do the right thing about the man who killed Hope. And heaven knows, you need him here with you."

"Sure, I'll do as you want. But who's going to ask if I've seen you?" Emma helped Wynoma lift the Dutch oven off the cast-iron stove.

"I don't know. Maybe no one. But I've got to be certain I'm without suspicion, that McAlistair doesn't think I know anything about that marshal. He just might send someone out here to check up on my story. Think you can handle it?"

Emma laughed. "What kind of fool question

is that, Wynoma Webster? I married Harry, didn't I? Anyone who can handle him can handle the worst McAlistair can send out here."

"Thanks." Hugging Emma, Wynoma thought of how much the women did to help each other out. Some men did the same, but with women there was another, special need to share things that men just couldn't be counted on to understand. Didn't matter what their color, they all knew they could depend on each other when it counted.

"I'll be heading back for town, then. Now, you send Harry on in, even if you get the slightest pangs there. Remember, once yours start coming, they pop out like peas from pods!"

"I remember!" Hugging each other, they laughed.

"Doesn't seem right, does it, that we have to do all this lying to get the man who killed Hope brought to justice?" Wynoma retied her bonnet, pushing one wild piece of hair under its brim.

"Been going on too long, no real law in McAlistair. Hate to say it, but it's about time the Federal law got here. Just wish it had been sooner." Emma shook her head.

Looping the excess reins in her palms, Wynoma backed up the mule and wagon. "Guess this has been a long time coming. Still, I'd rather it wasn't this particular marshal who had to do the dirty work. Reckon I've grown a bit partial to him, right fast. And I certainly don't want

Tyler in this at all. Figure it's my Christian duty to do all I can."

Emma smiled up at her friend. "So, there is more to this than just seeing justice done. Well, God go with you, Wynoma. If you need help, you let me know."

"I think I'm the one to be saying that to you, Emma." Waving good-bye, she cracked the old whip on Beulah and headed back to town.

Vera scrubbed the pine table in the kitchen, her face creased with worry as she pushed the brush into the grain. It was a puzzle, how she was going to warn Wynoma that McAlistair was watching out for her to get back to town. Absorbed in her mindless, methodical task, she didn't hear the back door creak open.

"Vera, it's me." Wynoma stepped warily into her own kitchen. "Any customers?"

Dropping the brush with a clatter, Vera stood stock-still. "Lordy, Miss Wynoma, you sure gave me a good fright. Here I am, all in a dither about how I'm going to find you and let you know we've got trouble in a big way, and you come creeping up behind me!"

"I wasn't creeping. What kind of trouble?" With a sigh, Wynoma pulled out the lone chair by the cookstove and reached down to unlace her boots. It was too hot for shoes today, and she'd been going since before dawn.

Vera disappeared into the front, returning with

a chair. "Locked the door. Don't need no more of McAlistair's men around here—we've got bucketsful as it is."

"What do you mean? They been bothering you 'cause I've been out of town? Everyone knows I always stay away a week or so with a birthing."

Vera unwrapped the bandanna she'd used to tie back her black, straight hair as she cleaned up the kitchen. "Who else? Anyone, everyone who works for McAlistair. It got noticed, it did, you leaving town and that Federal Marshal disappearing on the same day. McAlistair sent his dogs after him that morning, planning on finishing up what they'd started so the whole town could see how much he respected the law, and lo and behold, the marshal's gone, and no one to see where he's off to. So the sheriff and those sidekicks of McAlistair's start counting heads, asking around, and come to find out you and the wagon lit out that night. Asked me where you went off to, and I told 'em, just like you said, to bring a baby into this world of woe."

Pausing, Vera used the bandanna to wipe her broad face. "Don't mind telling you, they scared me silly. That night, when the marshal got into it here with McAlistair's men—well, I was right frightened then, but nothing like now. They let me know, they did, that if'n you went off to help the law, they'd make us sorry for it."

Wynoma wearily wiped a finger over the cast-iron surface of the stove. "Needs lye. I'll get to it next."

"You hear me, Miss Wynoma? They're looking for you, and there isn't a man jack here who'll do anything to stop them."

"I hear you. Now quit worrying. We got work to do before dinner. I don't see anything cooking yet." Standing, Wynoma reached for her apron, tying it in big, quick knots behind her.

Vera stood, slack-jawed, as Wynoma pulled from the open shelves tins of flour, salt, baking powder. "Miss Wynoma, I don't intend on standing by, watching what those men do to you. If you don't have the common sense God gave a goose, I'm not going to be here when they come."

Turning violently, Wynoma let fly a wide arc of flour from the spoon in her hand. "And I ain't asking you to. If you want to git, git."

Backing away, Vera let her apron drop. Large tears streaked her brown face as she stumbled out the back door. Wynoma threw the latch behind her.

"Good," she mumbled aloud. "Now she's out of the way, I can do some planning." It would be safer for Vera to go home for a while, and she knew it all too well. The night they'd held Vera hostage would pale in comparison with what was to come. It wouldn't matter to McAlistair that they were women.

Wynoma checked the contents of an old flour tin. She unwrapped the oily cloth inside and let the gun fall into her lap. Holding the small, well-oiled revolver in the palm of her hand, she checked its chambers. She'd use it if she had to. *Lord,* she prayed, *forgive me for doing this. Thou shalt not kill, but sometimes, Lord, it looks like it's the only way of doing the right thing.*

She returned the revolver to the tin. It was time to be getting dinner ready. Her regular clientele would be showing up in an hour or so. Just how long it would take McAlistair to find out she was back in town remained to be seen, but she was betting he wouldn't make his move until most people had gone and she started to close up for the night. She'd be ready.

Chapter Eleven

THE campfire felt good. Warming his hands on the battered mug, Moses watched Tyler drift off to sleep, his head cradled in his arms. Quanta, too, watched the boy.

"You're a fool, and you'll die for it." Quanta spit out the words. "Him too. I should have killed him the first time."

"Thought you'd want to sell the likes of him, Quanta. Must have been slipping, to let a white woman and boy almost get the better of you."

"No one gets the better of Juan Quanta, you pig. I do what I want, go where I want, take what I want."

Gesturing with his mug at the tied wrists, Moses couldn't suppress a grin. "Sure, like that, all trussed up, you don't let anyone best you. Seems to me, that boy there would've gotten you first if I hadn't made him hang back. Your sort always ends up on the short end of a rope or face down in the dirt."

The *pistolero*'s black eyes bored into Moses, who could almost feel the heat of their malevolence. "I been figuring on it, and there's something else going on here. That boy ain't it. All I got left to figure with is that widow woman, the one who took in that boy. I been watching her a right long time now on my way back to McAlistair, and I know when a woman gets to needing a real man. So I took me a little detour." The gunman leered at the disgust on Moses' face.

"So I been gettin' straight what happened. You and that boy seem right thick. Musta knowed each other real well. So I say to myself, how'd he get to know that boy? Well, I tell myself, the marshal's been visiting with the lady. And that's why you're so all fired up about her, right, Marshal? You like that woman real particular?" Snorting with derision, Quanta leaned over closer to Moses. "What did she think of you, Señor Marshal?"

Snapping his hand onto the slaver's windpipe, Moses started to squeeze. Gasping as he twisted away, Quanta floundered like a fish fighting the hook. "You been thinking too much. Not good for a no-mind lowlife like you, Quanta. So you take care how you voice your opinions, or I'll think of finishing it right here and now. When mad dogs like you get to drooling down the streets, only thing left is to shoot you out of your misery."

Tyler stirred and opened one sleepy eye. "Hmmm?" he queried sleepily. "Want me to sit guard, Marshal?"

Moses kneaded his fingers in his palm. "No need, Tyler. You go on back to sleep, hear?"

The boy rolled over on his side, fatigue forcing his body into rest. Moses leaned over, pulling the saddle blanket over the boy's shoulders.

"Only reason I don't end it here, Quanta, is I want the satisfaction of seeing you swing. It's a hard way to die, and the only one you're deserving of after what you did to Hope Hamill. Yessiree, the law'll give you just what you deserve. And maybe it'll put this boy's mind to rest, once and for all."

Quanta rolled onto his back, his wrists crossed on his chest. "You got a long way to go to Fort Smith. And my money's on me." His eyes closed, and he appeared to fall into an instant sleep.

"Yeah, well you've lost it this time." Moses was angry at himself for being drawn into this senseless repartee. But the truth was, he was on edge. His sixth sense had been screaming loud and long for the last day and a half, and it had nothing to do with getting to McAlistair. If he could have just tied Quanta up and left him, it would have been worth the time to double back, check to see if they were being followed. But he had to get to the town before McAlistair began to have suspicions about Quanta's failure to return from the market and sent out some of his men to look for the gunman. Moses didn't need to let them pick the place and time. And he had to check on Wynoma. He worried in silence, the boy's deep, even breathing and Quanta's snoring ignored for the moment. He concentrated on the nagging at the back of his mind that he hadn't had time to think about since capturing Quanta.

As the hours passed, the itching in his sixth sense got worse. He knew he had to check it out or he'd never get any rest. He kicked the fire low.

"Tyler, you awake?" Gently shaking the boy's shoulder, he waited for a sleepy response. Instead, Tyler was instantly awake and reaching for the old Betsy.

"Yes, sir, sure am." Stretching for his boots, Tyler stood.

"Hold on just a minute. I want to talk with you. Seems like we got someone dogging us, and I need to play a little trick to find out just who it is. Think you can help?"

"Try me." Grimly determined, Tyler started to poke Quanta.

"Leave him be." Holding the barrel of the shotgun, Moses gestured for silence. "I'm going to have to get out of camp without whoever's out there knowing. Make it look like you're still under that blanket. I'll give you my hat and all, and you sit where I've been guarding Quanta, only pull the brim down low, look like you're snoring some. Keep still now, while I cut the fire down to nothing, and then you build it back up, make sure they see you from out there. I'll be back in about five hours, at least just after dawn. And if I don't make it back, you leave Quanta here, ride out on Chloe, and get to Miss Wynoma, you hear?"

"But you're coming back. Why wouldn't you?"

"Never know, Tyler. Might just fall down a rabbit hole." His voice was gruff, but inside he wanted to hold the boy's thin shoulders between his hands and make sure he understood how dangerous it was for him to pose as the marshal. But that wouldn't change the fact that it had to be done and that Tyler would balk at any show of affection.

"Ready?" As Tyler nodded, Moses kicked the fire even lower, the dirt smothering most of it. Quietly, they exchanged hats and positions. Assuming Moses' position, Tyler let his chin sink to his chest.

Slipping into the shadows, Moses paused to assess the sounds of the night. Dawn was about four hours away, and he'd have to move fast and on foot. He'd move faster with Chloe, but he couldn't risk the noise. Setting out at a steady trot, he headed south of their camp. If they'd been followed, it had to be by someone who'd sniffed them out at the border.

His night vision was acute after all the years spent hunting along the James River. With his sharpened sense of hearing, he excluded the usual rustlings of rabbits and the tumble of pebbles from beneath his boots and concentrated, but it was the scent of horse that let him know he was right in the first place. About four miles from their camp, he heard the soft crackle of brush beneath a shifting hoof and the snort of one dozing animal to another. Dropping to the ground, he elbowed forward.

Cursing his stupidity in not noticing them on his trail, he wondered who they were, and how many. The boy had been vocal, too vocal, in the cantina, and heaven knew who could have followed Tyler from the town when he'd lit out after him. Inching forward until he was able to see the pale light of their campfire, he settled down into the dirt and waited.

The deep indigo of the night was broken only by the stars. Looking up, he sighted north and calculated how much farther they had to go. They were too close to McAlistair to be careless. As morning approached, he counted the shapes beside the fire and was surprised at their number. Five of them—which could mean only one thing: trouble. This was no casual cowhand looking for work, a lone gunhawk riding the border towns. Men banded together, far from any *ranchero,* McAlistair's types.

After thinking briefly of trying to take them all, he dismissed the thought. Not with the boy in tow. He couldn't face the risk of having anything happen to Tyler. It was bad enough with Quanta, but he could handle that. For a second, he was surprised at his strong attachment to Tyler and the fatherly feelings that had forced

On the Terror Trail

their way to the surface. Tyler was his prime consideration, and he reluctantly acknowledged it.

Soft streaks of violet and gold cut across the horizon as he began working his way back to their camp. Quietly picking up his pace, he pushed faster than he should have on the uneven, unknown terrain. A searing pain ripped through his ankle as he felt his foot wedge between rocks, and he fell hard on his side. *Stars and bars!* he cursed silently, as his ribs competed with his ankle for attention. Reaching down to check on the leg, he didn't feel the footsteps approach.

"Well, lookee here, what do we have? Got ourselves a mighty big rabbit for breakfast, I do believe."

Twisting aside in one violent thrust, Moses pulled his gun. Shots blazed out in the dawn, lead thudded into flesh. The sun rose lazily into the pale blue of morning.

Chapter Twelve

WYNOMA smoothed back her hair and gave an extra tug on her apron bow. Swishing through the door from her kitchen, she gave a broad smile to the two men sitting in the café.

"Evening, gents. We've got some fresh beef stew tonight, or maybe you'd like a fried steak?"

It was too hot for the heavy leather vest worn by the one with the silver conchos on his hat. But the flat, dark face of the gunhawk was as cold as ice. Toying with the spoon at his place, he set it clattering across the planks like a child's top. Wynoma jumped.

"So, what'll it be, boys?" She tried to keep her tone of voice calm, almost bored by their menacing looks.

"McAlistair wants you, now." Standing, the tall one with his hair hanging over his eyes dropped his hand to his gunbelt.

"Why?" Hands on hips, Wynoma returned his stare.

Hand snaking out, the one with the vest pulled Wynoma's wrist behind her with a wrench that made her want to scream.

Biting her lips, she forced a smile. "Now, no need to get rough, boys. It's just that I've got a business to run here, and I'm the only one doing the cooking tonight. Tell Mr. McAlistair I'll get over to see him soon as I close up."

The gunhawk increased the pain on her wrist. "Now, and don't make no more fuss, or I'll make sure you don't use this arm again."

"All right, all right. Just let me get my apron off, I'll be right back." She thought desperately of the old six-shooter in the flour tin.

"Uh-uh. Move it." Forcing her from behind, the one with the vest pushed her toward the door.

"So let go. How am I supposed to walk with you jerking me all over the place?" Wynoma tried to pull free and fought down the desire to kick him in the groin. If she didn't play the scene right this time, there wouldn't be a second chance.

McAlistair was holding court in the back room of the saloon. A desultory game of poker continued as Wynoma stood, hot and flushed, flanked by the gunmen, behind McAlistair's chair.

Discarding a card, he took another, and looked from his hand around his shoulder. "Don't like people watching over my back when I'm playing cards."

The gunhawks pulled her to the side. "We brought her like you said, boss."

Wynoma felt like a pigeon about to be used as

hawk bait. "What's this all about? I've got a café to run, and your men here just dragged me out of my kitchen with no explanation, no nothing. Now see here, I'm heading back for my place right now if I don't get some answers." Keeping her voice filled with righteous indignation, she knew her innocence was still a question mark. Otherwise, she'd have been dead already.

McAlistair spread his hand on the table. "Looks like my straight wins, gents. Now, who's buying the next round?" Almost casually, he leaned back in the chair and stared briefly into Wynoma's eyes. She felt the fear stir in her stomach like churning buttermilk. One of the gunfighters headed for the bar.

"So what's the problem, gentlemen? Want a change in menu? Or maybe different dinner hours?" The false bravado in her voice sounded like a tin bell to her ears.

The gunfighter stopped beside her and gave her a longing look. "Can I have her, boss?"

"Shaddup. Clear out, the lot of you."

They all vanished like ice before a fire. Wynoma folded her arms and waited, the trembling in her hidden for the moment. Dealing with McAlistair would be like sidestepping a striking rattler.

"You been taking any trips lately, Miss Wynoma? Haven't been able to get any of your good coffee these past few days, so I had my people do some checking. Seems like Vera didn't quite know where you were."

"You know I do birthings, Mr. McAlistair. Had to check on one of my ladies—she usually comes early. What's the problem?"

McAlistair pulled a cheroot from his vest pocket and lit it. "Um. Who's expecting? Not a certain U.S. Marshal, I think."

"What's the difference who it was? You wouldn't know her anyway. Why're you asking me about that marshal? He's been gone for weeks, way I hear it."

"Any idea where he went, Wynoma? Did you take him to some of your people? Now, look here, I don't want to hurt you, but I'm getting a real strong feeling that you aren't being exactly truthful. I won't stand for that." Jabbing the burning cheroot in his whisky glass, he reached for Wynoma's chin, holding it with fingers like steel.

Wynoma met his gaze firmly, consciously willing all fear to leave her. "Her name's Emma. Emma Gonzales. If you want to drive out to talk with her, be my guest. Or you can ride along with me in another week or so—she'll be ready then. Ever helped with a birthing, Mr. McAlistair?" She barely kept the sarcasm from her voice. "If you've got anything else you want to know, you come ask me yourself. No need to send your dogs after me."

Stepping back, he checked his pocket watch. "I don't believe you, Wynoma. But don't worry,

I'll be watching. And if you make a mistake, I'll get you. You and your friend." Running his finger along the bottom of her throat, he circled it with his hand. "And when you do, I'll make sure the both of you learn your lessons. No one tries to fool me, not in my own town they don't."

Her blood was hot with anger. "You don't own me, McAlistair. No one owns me now, or ever again." Turning on her heel, she marched for the door of the saloon. "Tell your men to stay out of my place. They ain't welcome, and I've got a gun that'll tell them so."

His laughter rang out behind her as she strode across the street. Both of them knew her threat was hollow. But she was still alive.

Chapter Thirteen

MOSES fought off the gray fog that threatened to keep him inundated in waves of unconsciousness. Pulling his eyes open, he found he could see nothing at first. Then it hit him. The pain washed over him from head to toe like a storm from the mountains, leaving him chilled and in agony.

"That's a tough one for sure. Lookee here, boys, we've got ourselves real buzzard bait!" The twang of the speaker cut through Moses' concentration. Slowly, he found himself staring at the scarred chin and beady eyes of a *pistolero.*

"Hughhh." He tried to clear the muck from his throat. "Water." The words were barely distinguishable, even to him. Trying to salivate, he realized his mouth tasted like bitter metal and his lips were caked in dried blood.

"Think we oughta waste any on this old bird?" The one with the scar chortled at Moses' attempts to sit upright.

"Shoot, might as well. Won't be no fun if we can't hear him scream."

Holding the old leather water pouch to his lips,

the bandit gave him just a swallow. "No sense wasting much on you, buzzard bait. Now, what ya doing coming after us, and how'd you find our trail? Come on, Marshal"—he slurred the last word like a man calling a favorite hound—"speak up nice and pretty so we can all hear you."

"Who're you?" Moses managed to form the words, but barely.

"Well, seems like maybe we done made a mistake." Picking at his gums with a pocketknife, another of the *pistoleros* watched with amusement as Moses sat up, shaking his wounded head to clear the grogginess. "Why, Marshal, you've gone and killed us a real good friend, and now you say you don't even know who we are? And you expect us to believe that?"

They laughed derisively. "I know, it just so happens you were heading for a Sunday social when you happened to find us. Right, Marshal?"

It came back to him suddenly, the twisted ankle, the shots in the early light of dawn. "You belong to McAlistair?" He figured the head wound was superficial or he'd be in a lot worse shape. Scalp wounds bled pretty badly, but weren't necessarily fatal. The knotted rope hogtying him was worse. Wiggling upright, he spat out some of the dried blood.

"We don't give answers, Mr. Marshal, until we get some. Why are you on our trail?"

"I'm not. Figured you were dogging me, so I

came on back to check it out. I'm not after any of you, just McAlistair."

"So, is that the boss man in the Territory? We're aiming to sign on somewhere." The four men looked at one another expectantly. "Looks like we done found ourselves a way in. Guess if you want this McAlistair so badly, he must want you too. Got ourselves a little present, so to speak."

"Wait a minute." Moses was thinking fast. "Maybe we can do a little bargaining here."

"Bargain, that's a good one." One of the *pistoleros,* the one with the Indian eyes, flipped out his gun. "He killed Blake. I say we get rid of him now."

"Not so fast, Julio."

Moses watched the four, gauging their relationship with one another. "Let's do some talking, and maybe we can work something out. I'll go on my way, you go on yours, and we'll leave it at that. Nothing personal about Blake, but he was just in the wrong place at the wrong time."

He hoped he was buying time, time for Tyler to get the heck out of there. Because once the *pistoleros* decided a course of action, they'd take it without mercy. And Tyler would be right in their way. He'd totally forgotten about Quanta.

"But he's the law!" one of them protested violently.

"And killing a Federal Marshal will make you marked men for sure. Be sensible, let me go, and

I'll forget I ever saw you." He wondered how long he'd been gone from the camp. Squinting at the sun, he figured it was an hour after he'd told Tyler he'd be back.

"I say we take him with us. If McAlistair wants to get him as badly as he wants to get McAlistair, we got ourselves a real good start. I say we throw him on Blake's horse and ride."

"Say, where's his mount? Gotta be somewhere." They looked vaguely about the country. "Don't suppose there's more of them out there, do you?"

"Nope, I'm alone—no one with me." As soon as he spoke, Moses knew he should have kept his mouth shut.

"Well, what do you know. Saddle up, Julio. Let's go do some checking around." Julio moved toward the picketed horses.

"Waste of time." Moses spat out the words. "McAlistair will pay good money for me. You want to turn a profit quick here, you'd better ride out now."

They looked from one to the other. "Sounds good to me." The one called Julio threw a bridle on a flashy Appaloosa.

"So what're we waiting around for? Been looking for something for days, now we got it, let's ride."

Scar-chin nodded in agreement, cinching a bay that was chewing on a wad of grass. "We ain't far now. All we got to do is show our faces, hand over this here lawman, and we're in. I 'spect we just might end up rich men, *hombres.*"

Their laughter carried. Thrown stomach-first over the gray that had belonged to the dead Blake, Moses prayed that Tyler hadn't come looking. It would mean Tyler's death for sure, and that was the one thing he couldn't stand to have happen.

Tyler knew it had been too long. The *pistolero* grinned at him with hungry eyes, and Tyler sensed from Quanta's careless slouch that he'd give him a hard time about moving out. Still, he was going to do what the marshal had said. Never again would he disobey Leland Moses.

"On your feet." Waving old Betsy at Quanta, Tyler stood. "And no tricks."

Quanta laughed. "You, boy—you think you're going to get me to Fort Smith alone. Aye, *muchacho,* you have much to learn. Too bad I didn't kill you. It would have saved you much trouble."

"Another word, and I'll gag you." Tyler's voice was cold with fury. But he knew he'd have to work fast or Quanta would seize every little opportunity to wear him down. And he was worried about the marshal.

"Get mounted." Snapping the order, Tyler watched Quanta saunter over to his mount. "Be quick about it."

"But how can I mount with my hands like

this?" Holding forth his manacled wrists, Quanta played the innocent. Tyler thought briefly of giving him a leg up, and knew instantly it was a trap.

"Get up by yourself, or you walk." Throwing his leg over the mule, Tyler grabbed Chloe's bridle with that of Quanta's horse. Shoving in his heels, he pulled out with the two horses behind him, Quanta hopping along with one foot in the stirrup.

Glancing at their camp and where the horses and mule had grazed, Tyler wondered briefly how the marshal would find them if they left him, on foot, out in this vast expanse of nothingness. But he knew it had to be done. This time he'd obey orders. He forced the mule forward, Quanta cursing obscenely behind him.

Just as they approached another small stand of cottonwoods, Tyler knew he wouldn't be able to live with himself if he kept on. Visions of the marshal, half dead in the grass and wondering where Tyler was, interfered with his sense of direction. He couldn't help it if he was going in circles and ended up doubling back to their camp of the night before. At least, that was how he rationalized his explanation to the marshal. If the marshal was still alive, he'd be mad as a wet hen, but it was the only excuse Tyler would give him. After that, he'd tell him the truth.

Gesturing for Quanta to dismount, Tyler kept his distance, the old shotgun aimed at the gunman's midsection. "Walk on over there, to them trees." Quanta stumbled as he landed on the ground, pretending to fall. "And no tricks. I'd just as soon shoot you now as later."

Quanta straightened, his oily black eyes slit like a snake's, waiting for the right moment to strike. "So what now, little *muchacho?* You make camp early, no, and wait for the marshal? Do not wait long, for he is dead, I am sure of it."

Pulling a lariat from the marshal's gear, Tyler made a quick slipknot, and looped the finely braided leather around Quanta's shoulders. He gave it a quick jerk and felt Quanta grunt as the air was squeezed out of him.

"Over here." Giving the end of the lariat a tug, Tyler led Quanta over to the thickest of the cottonwoods. A soft, hot morning breeze ruffled the leaves, exposing their silver undersides. Tyler forced Quanta to sit, legs spread around the trunk of the tree, while he bound him hand and foot in the awkward position. Giving his knots one extra jerk, Tyler stood back to survey his handiwork.

"If'n I don't come back for you, Quanta, just remember how you killed Miss Hope. I hope the critters eat you alive."

Swinging up on the mule, Tyler stopped. He'd be able to move faster on the marshal's mare, but he didn't want to leave anything for Quanta to ride, in the unlikely event he should manage to wiggle free. Scrambling onto Chloe's back, he pulled on the reins of the mule and Quanta's horse. "Come on, old girl." Clicking at the animals softly, he coaxed them into following Chloe. He'd find a safe place to stash them both, and then he'd be free to ride back to where the marshal had disappeared into the night.

Knowing that he'd be able to return to their previous night's camp more easily than scouting over unknown terrain, Tyler hobbled the mule loosely in the general vicinity of their old camp. "Now you be good, hear? I'll pick you up on the way back with the marshal, so you get yourself a bellyful, 'cause it'll be hard going from here to Fort Smith." Rubbing the mule between the ears, Tyler intently searched the horizon. There was something or someone out there who'd stopped the marshal from returning to camp, and it or they had to be dangerous.

Realizing he'd track better on foot, he set his sights for the direction the marshal had taken last night, and left the mule braying softly as they disappeared into the distance. Chloe followed, her reins looped over his shoulder, her head down as though she, too, sought tracks.

The signs were still fresh enough to follow. Eyes downcast, Tyler did a shuffling jog, his boyhood training chasing rabbits standing him in good stead. Still, his lungs began to burn when he heard the first sounds of the horses. Pulling to a quick halt, he moved to cover Chloe's muzzle to prevent her from greeting them. After jerking her behind a small outcropping, he crawled around the corner to listen more intently.

"Hey, Julio, I still say we double back, find out if there's any more of them where this one came from. Like as not, they'll be missing him by now, and we'll find ourselves surrounded by a necktie party by noon."

"Ain't no bunch of lawmen come riding down on us, less'n we done lost all our senses. Lordy, you can see for miles out here." Gesturing at the broad expanse of the terrain, the outlaw grinned at Moses.

" 'Course, this one does stick out like a sore thumb." They guffawed at the small joke.

From his hiding place behind the small outcropping Tyler heard the burst of laughter. Slipping into the saddle, he pulled out the shotgun and laid it across the saddle horn. He kicked Chloe's ribs and loped in the direction of the sound.

Cantering into the outer perimeter of the outlaws, Tyler put on his most innocent expression, the one Miss Hope had known meant he'd been into something bad. "Howdy there," he called out in a friendly fashion. "Where y'all heading?"

Moses' head jerked up and he twisted at his bonds. Tyler nodded in his direction. "You a posse? Looks like you done got yourself a big one. We done heard about some bad-gun types coming up from Mexico. My pa said to watch out when I took old Betsy rabbit hunting, guess I can tell him now you all done taken all the fun out of it for me. I was hoping to get myself a reward, I was."

Their hands on their gun butts, the outlaws listened to Tyler's monologue, all eyes on the shotgun.

"Where you hail from, boy?" Scar-chin kept his eyes on the shotgun.

"Over yonder. Been hunting. Ain't got a thing yet." Tyler was acting younger than his actual years. With his freckles and innocent expression, he was doing a credible job of lulling the *pistoleros* into dismissing him as nothing more than a boy out rabbit hunting.

"So, where you taking the prisoner, Fort Smith? I ain't never been there, but one of these days my pa and me, we're going to go for a week or so, watch a hanging, and...." Tyler chattered on as the outlaws grew restless and began turning their backs to him so that he would ride away.

Moses could see the released safety and Tyler's fingers curling around the triggers for the two barrels. Edging out of the outlaws' direct line of vision, Tyler moved Chloe closer to the marshal.

"Get on home, boy. Never know, some more of this here wanted man's friends might just be riding around, looking for him. They might think you helped us capture him. So get." Spurring their horses, the *pistoleros* trotted away from Tyler.

The first shotgun blast ripped through the

right arm and shoulder of the lead man. Spinning out of the saddle, he screamed as the others whirled to see where the attack was coming from. Swinging low in the saddle, Tyler pulled his rabbit knife and sawed at the ropes binding Moses. Shots cut through the air in all directions, as the dust rose and obscured the outlaws' line of vision.

"Where'd it come from, Julio?" Scar-chin screamed as he fired wildly. The horses shrieked as bits cut into their soft mouths and spurs raked them in circles.

Moses fell to the ground, hitting on his feet at a run for the horse of the shot outlaw. Just as Tyler stood in the stirrups to fire the second barrel, Moses found the rifle and snapped it into action. One more fell, wounded and howling, trying to hang on to his horse as he writhed in pain. Tyler, reaching for more shells in his pockets, saw Moses fling himself into a saddle.

Now that the *pistoleros* knew that Tyler was their enemy, the surviving outlaws whirled to fire. Moses saw Tyler freeze as he realized his situation. Giving the whistle that would bring Chloe at a run, Moses used the butt of the rifle against the horse's flanks to chase down the two still aiming for Tyler.

Crashing into the Appaloosa, Moses raked the rider's face with the sight end of the rifle. Snapping the weapon to his shoulder, he tried to aim at the other rider, but he found himself being grabbed from behind. Just as the rider toppled out of the saddle, another shotgun blast tore into the air, and he heard the curses of the man dragging him into the dirt.

Tyler pushed Chloe into the melee, his rabbit-hunting knife in his hand, Indian style. Just as Julio took aim, Moses grabbed the knife from Tyler, throwing it and hitting the outlaw low in the belly. With a scream, Julio dropped the pistol and clutched his abdomen. Tyler stared at the blood oozing slowly between the *pistolero*'s fingers, and turned pale. It was all over.

"It's okay, Tyler, just help me up, will you?"

Tyler pulled his eyes away from the man swaying in the saddle and jumped down from Chloe. As he reached for Moses' hands, the marshal pulled the boy to him in a bear hug. "You did fine, boy, just fine. Made a right smart back-up man, if I do say so myself."

Tyler said nothing, hiding his face in the marshal's shirt as the wounded outlaws groaned.

Releasing Tyler, Moses took the precaution of picking up all the weapons. "They won't be needing these anymore. What do you say, Tyler?"

Tyler nodded an assent. "I left Quanta back about ten miles, tied to a tree. What're we going to do with them?"

Moses knelt beside the worst of the lot and felt for a pulse. "Don't think we'll have to worry about them. They're goners, most of them." He rolled the shoulder-shot outlaw over and jerked him up. "This one can ride. We'll take him to Fort Smith, give Quanta some company."

Nodding, Tyler gathered in Chloe's reins. "You want to ride her, Marshal?" He looked forlornly at the bodies littering the ground, horses shuffling past them with reins dangling.

"No, you ride her, Tyler. You did just fine. Don't go worrying." Moses knew the carnage was eating at the boy. "It's better to feel like you do, Tyler, than to be happy about this. I'm proud of you, boy."

A faint smile crossed Tyler's face as he thrust his toe into the stirrup and swung his leg over the cantle. "I swore I'd never let this happen again, Marshal. Have my people killed, taken from me by scum like this."

"I know, Tyler, I know." Moses lifted up the moaning *pistolero,* tying his hands to the horn. What mattered was that Tyler felt the same strong bond that he felt. Getting Quanta and the rest of the scum to Fort Smith wasn't what really mattered, when he weighed his priorities. Tyler and Wynoma tipped the scale more than he'd have ever imagined they could.

Chapter Fourteen

WYNOMA watched the men with low-slung gunbelts and travel-tired horses pour into town. There wasn't much talk in her café these days since McAlistair had sent down word that she was to be watched. Still, she served his henchmen their lone cups of coffee as they sat for hours at her small tables, following her every move with eyes that appeared unblinking. It was starting to get on her nerves, but she reminded herself that she couldn't have a fit of hysteria until this whole thing was over, one way or another. Then she promised herself a nice, long crying jag.

Vera, too, was being followed, so Wynoma couldn't send any messages by her. Knowing her only hope for helping the marshal was in finding him before he ran into any traps, she took to riding out often, visiting houses where women were expecting, and then taking the long way home. Often, her ominous escorts stayed out of sight, but most of the time they rode right where she could see them. One day she'd had enough.

Pulling Beulah to a halt, she climbed down

from the wagon and trudged back to her follower. He halted as she approached.

Shading her eyes with the edge of her hand, she peered up into his hard, sun-lined face. "Howdy. Long way from town, aren't you?"

Leaning back in the saddle, the gunhawk rested the heel of his palm on the gun butt protruding from the well-oiled holster. His silence continued as she waited for a response.

"I want to know why you're following me. Seems like I can't go to the outhouse without an escort. Why?"

He leered down at her, his black teeth showing in his crooked grin. "Just go on about your business, if you know what's good for you. Then again, seems like you ain't so smart about what's good for you."

She huffed back to the wagon, clambering up with muttered curses under her breath. She hadn't expected a straight answer, just the satisfaction of bearding one of the lion cubs in its den. A lot of good it had done her. Still smarting from his condescending airs, she snapped the reins on Beulah's back.

The same man was with her when she visited the people who'd cared for Chloe. Watching him from the window of the small house, she shuddered.

"Miss Wynoma, come away from there. Won't do you no good, staring back." Taking her by the shoulders, Pedro Sanchez pulled her to the one fancy chair in the home. "Tyler'll know where they can hole up, if'n they need to. Heaven knows, that boy used to roam the country from one end to the other."

"I know, Pedro, I know. And the marshal did find your place when he got his horse. Still, if I don't know what he's thinking of doing, there's no way I can get up any help."

The large-boned man hunkered down by the hearth and pulled a plug of tobacco from his shirt pocket. He bit off a chunk and said, "Now, Wynoma, a black man wearing a marshal's badge is bound to attract right much attention wherever he goes. Word'll get back to you, one way or the other, 'bout him and the boy, if'n the boy's with him."

Maria Sanchez wiped her hands on her apron. "He's right, Wynoma. But I sure wish you'd stay with us until it's all done and finished. McAlistair'll kill you soon as look at you. And if he don't, one of his gun-hungry boys will do it for him. Look how they're treating you, like a cheating wife. Danged if I'd stay in town with that kind of stuff and nonsense going on!"

Wynoma thought a moment. "You may have an idea there, Maria. If they can't find me, how can they know what I'm up to? McAlistair has so many men in town, it's no problem to send a few to keep track of me. But out here, why, he's sending only one at a time. Easy enough to fool one idiot, don't you think?"

On the Terror Trail   143

Sitting beside Wynoma, Maria smiled. "Now that's more like it. So you will stay awhile?"

Shaking her head, Wynoma traced the long lines on her palm. "Had a palm reader do me once. First, she read some tea leaves, said I'd be successful in business. But she wouldn't tell me anything about my hand, said she could only say I'd have a long life. Tried paying her more to find out what she'd seen, but she wouldn't take it. Maybe now I'll finally know."

Closing her palm in the pocket of her skirt, she stood. "I'd best make my plans. I'll be back tonight. Only, don't worry about a place for me to sleep. I'll just pretend I'm coming out here, then head back for Miss Hope's."

"Let me come with you, Wynoma." His brow furrowed, Pedro put a protective arm about her shoulders. His wife nodded affirmatively. "Yes, Wynoma, don't go alone."

Smiling at their concern, Wynoma tied on her sun hat. "Now, you all will be in enough trouble when McAlistair finds out I'm gone. I don't want to involve you any more than necessary. I can always shut up the café and move out, but you've got land. You have to stay."

They watched her leave, the *pistolero* mounting up to follow.

By nightfall, she was back with an old carpetbag in the wagon. Making sure the gunhawk heard her, she exclaimed loudly about the generosity of their offer to have her stay a few days.

"Land's sake, I'm tired of cooking!" She protested as Pedro carried in her bag.

Disgusted, the hired gun built a small fire and pulled out a battered coffeepot. He'd be danged if he'd do this anymore. Trailing after a woman's skirts was no kind of work for a man, and he'd let McAlistair know exactly what he thought tomorrow. Still muttering under his breath, he pulled down his hat and shut his eyes as night began to fall. The coffee was bitter and tasted of stale water. He knew McAlistair would just as soon kill him as make him trail the woman to the ends of the earth if he complained, so he let the stars know exactly what he thought of this kind of duty for a man who had once ridden with Quantrill.

After making sure her provisions were tied to Beulah's back, Wynoma dressed in her darkest clothes. Whispering her good-byes, she struck out for Hope Hamill's place. She knew in her heart that Tyler would go back there, even if the marshal went on to Fort Smith. She prayed that was the way it would happen. But she feared it wouldn't.

Even with the moon, it was slow going to the abandoned farm. Beulah was sure-footed and remarkably quiet, and with no saddle to creak, Wynoma was sure she'd gotten away undetected. After hiding Beulah in the ramshackle barn, she made it into the house just as dawn began streaking the sky. Peering out from behind the threadbare curtains, she searched the horizon for her follower. No one was in sight.

She slumped onto Hope's small bed and prayed. It had been long enough. One or both of them had to come back, and she would be there to provide the warning.

Chapter Fifteen

"WE can't take them back to town, not yet, Marshal." Tyler stuck to his guns, arguing with Moses about their next move. "We're going to have to move fast, stash these prisoners until we figure out the lay of the land."

Moses was proud of the boy's reasoning. He would have made a good soldier. Quanta twisted in the saddle, spoiling Moses' moment of reflection.

"Mistake, Moses. Leave us out here, and you've got no chips to bargain with. McAlistair'll kill you on sight without me."

The marshal knew what Quanta feared. If he left the outlaws tied and gagged, and didn't return, they probably wouldn't be found until after they'd died of thirst and exposure. It was a nice form of death for that kind of scum, he mused to himself. But still, the *pistolero* had spoken with a grain of truth in his oily words. If he showed up in town with the outlaws in tow, McAlistair's curiosity and pride would certainly be aroused. One element would buy him time; the other encouraged a stupid move on McAlistair's part.

Having made his decision, Moses gestured for Tyler to ride up next to him. Pulling Chloe down to a trot, he waited for Tyler to catch up. "Good idea, Tyler. But this time, I'll have to do it another way. I'll need you to find Miss Wynoma before we get to town and tell her to get out. I don't want her getting hurt in any gunplay. Think you can do that, and then let me know?"

Tyler nodded. His small hands caressed the neck of the mule. "Can I ride the Appaloosa? I'd move a little faster then."

Moses wanted to reach out and pat the boy's head, feel the soft brown hair, and pull the child to him for a hug. But he knew Tyler would only be embarrassed by such a gesture.

"Sure, good idea. I'll head for Mrs. Hamill's, meet you there by nightfall. Be careful," he added as Tyler jerked the outlaw from his horse. *Be careful of McAlistair,* he wanted to add, but didn't. Tyler understood the danger of their situation, but his youth still wrapped him in invincibility. Any warning would appear patronizing.

He watched Tyler tear off into the distance, then shut his eyes to make sure he remembered every outline of the boy's sun-browned face. He wanted it saved, just as he knew he could bring up Jamie's or Wynoma's face in his mind's eye any time he needed to see them.

With Tyler now a speck on the horizon, Moses turned toward Hope Hamill's place. At least he knew the terrain thereabouts, in case there was trouble. His instincts were tingling, and he once more checked the prisoners' bonds. As soon as Tyler got back, he'd face McAlistair in his own lair. Possibly, he'd die. But McAlistair had to know there was someone in the Territory who would take him on in front of his own men.

"This is stupid, eh, Marshal?" Quanta's eyes bored into the skyline, his face turned from Moses. "You will die, and we will die with you, since you can't afford to let us live. And if you don't kill us, McAlistair will get us in trying to get you. So why play this game out? Fold it in, let us go, and you go your way. What do you say?"

Moses hid a soft smile. Quanta was right. "Because I do things my way. Now shut up."

He could tell from the sheen on the man's face and the tight lines of pain at the corners of his lips that Quanta needed some of the drugs he'd been using. The withdrawal was making the outlaw's mind clear and cutting with the two-edged sword of truth.

"Yeah, shut up," snarled the man now riding Tyler's mule. "McAlistair'll take care of us after he gets that one."

Quanta laughed raggedly. "We know better, don't we, Marshal? Still, it is better to die by the gun."

"It's better not to die at all," Moses spat in return. "Now, quiet!"

He knew his worry for Tyler and Wynoma was

affecting his instincts. Blocking them out of his mind as much as possible, he mentally reviewed the outlines of the town, the places where McAlistair would be prepared for an ambush, where he might not. It was part of his routine, thinking out every move ahead of time, just in case it might work the way he wanted it to. Even when things went wrong, he was sometimes able to salvage what might have been a total loss, just because he'd planned it from the beginning.

It was late afternoon when he sighted the small, low house where Hope Hamill was now buried in the yard. Halting his prisoners half a mile from the place, he watched. Just as he had the first time he'd ridden in, he waited a bit before proceeding. He smelled the coffee before he saw any smoke from the chimney.

Someone had moved in and was waiting for them! Knowing he couldn't leave his prisoners behind, he was tempted to veer away and intercept Tyler on his way back from town. But an inhabitant at Hope Hamill's place could mean only one of two things: Either McAlistair had figured out what was going on and had sent a man to wait for and kill him in case he'd return there, or squatters had moved in. In either case, news of Hope's grave must be all over McAlistair.

Praying that the second option was the correct one, Moses forced the two men to ride before him. McAlistair's man wouldn't shoot Quanta without asking questions first, and squatters would never know the difference. Trotting into the dusty yard, Moses made sure he was shielded by the bodies of the two outlaws.

"Hello, the house!" he called out, his hat brim pulled low, rifle across the saddle horn. Swinging his eyes from the barn to the house, he figured there was one person only, and one not too well prepared at that. If it was one of McAlistair's men, it was a dumb one. They were a few feet from the porch, but anyone inside would have a hard time seeing him behind Quanta.

Just then a shotgun blast spit from the window by the door, and Moses dived from the saddle. Some of the buckshot winged the man riding the mule, and he slumped back over the rump of the animal. Quanta, with a grunt, fell forward onto the horse's withers and drove spurs into the horse, twirling in frantic circles as he tried to evade the next salvo.

"Hold your fire! We're friendly!" Moses called out as he dodged up to the door, his Colt in one hand, rifle in the other.

Just when he expected another spray of pellets from the broken glass, the door cracked open. Then a sudden whirlwind of gingham and strong brown arms flew into him as the door was flung wide. "Leland!" Wynoma cried out, her relief evident in every note of the name.

He held her tightly, afraid to speak. She was already safe. It was only then that he realized that the soreness in his neck and shoulders didn't come from the fight the other morning, but from carrying a load of worry for her.

"Wynoma, Wynoma," he repeated as she buried her face in his chest. "It's okay, Wynoma, I'm back. It's okay."

Just as he pulled her away from him to study her face, he felt Quanta making a break for it. Although bound hand and foot to the saddle, he was hunched low and spurring as though the devil were on his trail. Dropping to one knee, Moses took careful aim. The shot ripped squarely through Quanta's back.

Wynoma, her eyes teary with joy, put her hand to her mouth as she saw where the outlaw's horse was taking him. Terrified by the gunfire and the flopping body, the animal galloped across the small mound of dirt that covered Hope Hamill. "Oh, no!" she cried out. "Stop him, Leland. Stop him!"

Moses watched helplessly as the horse tore across the yard and hit open ground. "I'll pick him up when the horse tires. No sense in pushing Chloe any more than necessary. She's had a hard time of it as it is."

When the horse trotted back to the house at last, Moses knew Quanta was dead. Picking up the unconscious outlaw, he undid the ropes and let the *pistolero* slump to the ground. Checking the wounds from the buckshot, he saw they weren't bleeding too profusely. He turned to see Wynoma staring at him with panic in her eyes.

"Leland, where's Tyler?" Suddenly fearful, she was afraid he was dead.

He didn't want to tell her the truth.

Tyler edged into town the back way, keeping the Appaloosa off the main street. It was early morning, and the riffraff would, he knew, be drifting in for a long day of drink and gambling. Tying the horse to an empty stall, he looked around for the Mexican who kept the place mucked out.

Seeing the man in the grain room, Tyler inched to catch him before he was himself seen. "Psst, Tomas," he hissed, careful to keep his voice low in case some of McAlistair's men were around. "I need your help."

Startled, Tomas dropped the bucket of grain. "Boy, don't you ever go sneaking up on me that way again, or I'll have your hide!"

Tyler shut the door to the grain room. "Won't, I promise. I've gotta find Miss Wynoma. Know where she is? I don't want to go barging into the café and have everyone see me."

The old Mexican stepped back. "You in some kind of trouble, boy? Where's Miss Hope? What's going on here? You know Miss Wynoma's being watched by McAlistair. He thinks she knows where that marshal is, and he's going to catch her and him one of these days."

Holding his battered old hat by the edge of its brim, Tyler curled it between his palms. "Miss

On the Terror Trail 153

Hope's dead, Tomas. Slaver named Quanta, one of McAlistair's slavers, killed her. He thought he killed me too. I need to find Miss Wynoma." Tomas's words about Wynoma and McAlistair hadn't sunk in yet.

Tomas shook the boy by the shoulders. "You stay clear of her, hear me? I'll help you bury Miss Hope, and once things settle down, I'll get a wire off to Fort Smith. They'll send someone out after this here fella who killed her, so just quiet down."

"It's not that, Tomas. The marshal has him. Quanta, I mean. I'm supposed to find Miss Wynoma, tell her to get out of town. The marshal's coming after McAlistair!"

The Mexican's jaw dropped with surprise. "I don't believe it. The black man's alive? And coming in after McAlistair? I don't believe it!"

"Can you find Miss Wynoma and tell her? They won't be looking for you to tell her anything, Tomas." Tyler suddenly had a clear picture of what was going on. Wynoma was a marked woman, just as much as the marshal.

"I'll try, boy. You stay here. I'll see what I can find out."

Tyler watched from the back of the stable as the Mexican crossed the street and headed for Wynoma's café. Squatting down, he smelled the hot hay and ammonia of wet stalls and shut his eyes. If Wynoma wasn't there, if she was out on one of her birthing visits, he'd get out as soon as it was dark.

Tomas dog-trotted back to the livery, his face shining in the heat. "Boy, where are you?"

Tyler emerged from the shadows, his face eager with hope. "Did you find her and tell her what the marshal said?"

Shaking his head, the Mexican squatted beside Tyler. "She's gone. Vera says the place is closed for a while. She don't know when Wynoma's gonna be back."

Tyler felt his stomach sink. Now he'd have to look for her, and he didn't know where to start.

Moses and Wynoma stood, their eyes locked. "Where's Tyler?" Wynoma repeated. "He must have taken off after you!"

Moses sank wearily onto the sofa and pulled Wynoma down beside him. "He did. I sent him into town, to warn you. Figured you'd better get out before I came in after McAlistair, and that you two would be safer together, away from me."

He held her rough hand in his, stroking her fingers. "He's one smart boy, Wynoma. I love him like he's my own."

Squeezing his palm, Wynoma tried to reassure him. "He'll figure out where you are, get back here by morning, just you wait and see. Why, that boy can outfox the devil himself!"

Laughing in spite of the bleak situation, Moses pulled Wynoma to him. "And you—why, you mean as much to me as that boy. Just wanted to tell you that, in case I don't get a chance later."

On the Terror Trail

Wynoma kissed his hand. "Same here. Just in case I don't get a chance later." Echoing his words, she felt the full weight of their meaning.

"I did a lot of thinking. About you. About Tyler. What it'd be like to have a family, a home. Felt good. Never thought I'd feel that way. Haven't till now. Bad thing is, soon as I got to knowing I'd like to have that with you, I got careless. And I knew why I'd never let myself think that way before. It's dangerous for a man in my line of business. Can't be afraid to risk it all, or you're dead." He waited for the import of his words to sink in.

Wynoma frowned. "You proposing, Leland Moses?"

He laughed. "Guess I am." The laughter stopped. "But I've got to take in McAlistair before I quit. Chances are I won't make it. Just wanted you to know how I felt, I guess."

"Good enough for me, you fool. I accept!" Pulling him to her, she gave him a kiss. He held her close and knew he shouldn't have allowed himself to fall in love. It would make it all the harder to finish his job. Knowing what could have been his in life—the love and home he'd always wanted—drove fear for himself into his heart for the first time he could remember. He didn't want to give her up.

"Wynoma, please don't." He jerked free of her embrace. "When this is over. . . ." He left the rest unsaid.

Puzzled, she tried to kiss him once more. He suddenly stood up and marched across the room from her.

"This is no good. I'm a dead man, more than likely, and we both know it. And if I don't kill McAlistair, you're dead too. So promise me you'll leave at first light if Tyler isn't back."

Standing to face him, hands on hips, Wynoma could barely choke out the words. "No one tells me what to do, Leland Moses. And I'll do as I see fit, so don't go ordering me around. I'm not your wife yet!"

His face softened. "Wish you were."

"Well, it still wouldn't give you the right to tell me what to do, far as I'm concerned. And I'm staying. If you don't get McAlistair, I will."

He knew she meant it. "Don't be a fool! You're no match for the sidewinder! Save Tyler, get yourself as far from here as you can. I've got a bank account in St. Louis—I'll write you a draft for the balance. Take the money, set yourself up somewhere else, send Tyler to school."

"I can't be bought, Leland Moses!" Her tone was haughty.

He knew he'd blundered. "I'm not trying to buy you, Wynoma. It's just that— Well, I thought it'd make it easier for you. Starting over can be mighty hard. I know, I've done it."

"If there's to be any starting over, we'll do it together." She caught him in her arms. "You, me, Tyler. Why, we can get this place running again! Miss Hope just didn't have a man to help her—it's good soil! And Tyler'll want to stay. We'll send him to school if he wants, but I'm betting you can teach him, and me too. . . ."

He placed a finger on her lips. "Hush. Enough of dreams." He searched the room for signs of writing implements. A stubby pencil was on the mantel, next to a grocery list Hope Hamill had started before her death. Smoothing it out, he wrote the account number and the draft instructions on the back. "Suppose I should write out some kind of will too. Just in case you have trouble with the bank."

Wynoma looked at the paper. "What's it say?"

He read it to her. "Wish I had time to teach you to read and write, Wynoma." Folding the paper, he placed it in her hand. "There's so much I'd like to do with you." The loss he felt was as though she were dead to him already.

Sensing his drift, she placed her fists on his chest and moved closer. "We'll do it all. I just know it. I've got a long life line." She pointed to her palm. "And I intend on spending it with you."

" 'If wishes were horses. . . .' " he quoted.

"Not a wish, Marshal, just a fact. I'm not a fancy woman, and I've known some hard times. The past is the past and the dead are gone and buried, but we'll make it." What she really wanted to do was to beg and plead with him to wait for Tyler and then to walk away, leaving

McAlistair for someone else. She knew it would never work. The act of asking him would lessen her in his eyes, and she'd never do that. She'd take what she could get and treasure it forever.

They waited the night through, hands touching, sitting silently in the dark, afraid to say the things that would only be painful memories tomorrow. Moses wanted nothing more, he wanted everything, and the contradictions tore at him like fangs.

Chapter Sixteen

THE gunhawk sidled into the back room of the saloon, his eyes dark with anticipation. He waited for McAlistair to take two cards before speaking.

"Got something might interest you, Mr. McAlistair." He waited for permission to proceed. He knew this was worth his weight in gold; he wanted McAlistair's full attention. Might even earn himself a raise for this kind of information.

McAlistair raised the ante, then turned for a quick look at his hireling. "Better be good. What you got to tell me?" His voice was soft but deadly. No one interrupted his poker games.

"Been watching that place, Wynoma's, and I seen that old Mexican, one who cleans the livery, head in the back door. So I followed, put my ear right up there, and listened real good." Pausing for effect, the gunman could barely suppress a grin.

McAlistair called. The others bowed out of the game. Triumphantly hauling in the pot, McAlistair turned his thick-featured face toward the gunhawk. "So?"

"Seems the marshal sent that boy, the one Mrs. Hamill found, to town to find Wynoma. To warn her about him coming in after you, so she could get out afore the lead starts flying." He paused, proud of his succinct recitation.

"Why didn't you bring the boy with you?" McAlistair's eyes would have frozen a pond.

The gunhand blustered. "Well, I guess, I thought maybe . . . well, you might not want to tip him off. I think. . . ."

"I don't pay you to think. Bring him here, *now.*" The last word cut through the tension in the room like a knife. Everyone rose with McAlistair as he carefully placed his winnings in his pockets. "Good afternoon, gentlemen." With a disdainful nod at the lackeys he regularly cleaned out at the poker table, McAlistair led the way through the saloon. "I'll be in my office. Bring him there."

Without a backward glance, the Scotsman marched across the dusty street. The onlookers watched the gunhawk's eyes follow McAlistair into the false-front building. At a trot, he suddenly ran for the livery.

Rounding the corner of the stable, the gunhawk drew his pistol. "Hey you, stableboy! Come on out!"

Tyler heard the command and ducked for the stall with the Appaloosa. Gesturing for silence,

On the Terror Trail 161

the Mexican picked up a pitchfork. "Whatcha want?"

"Send out the boy, the one sent by that marshal. Mr. McAlistair wants to see him." Edging around the corner, the gunman waited for his eyes to adjust to the semidarkness of the livery. Motes of dust swirled in the air as his boots stirred the straw on the floor.

"What for?" Holding the pitchfork before him, the Mexican moved into the shadows.

"Nothing. Just wants to talk to him." Crouching, the gunhawk moved into the darkness, listening.

Tyler edged the horse to one side of the stall, trying to mount in silence. The Appaloosa turned in a circle, the saddle creaking loudly. "Whoa," he whispered in the horse's ears, tugging on the reins.

"Come on out, boy." The gunman moved to the stall, ignoring the Mexican.

Suddenly, with a swish, the pitchfork cut through the air and sliced into the gunhawk's arms.

"Arrgh!" His scream ripped out.

"Go, Tyler!" Kicking the weapon from the gunman, the Mexican flung wide the stall door.

One toe in the stirrup, Tyler grabbed a handful of mane and clicked at the Appaloosa. He ducked through the door as the Appaloosa cantered into the daylight. Trying to gather in the reins, Tyler leaned low in the saddle. He knew all too well why McAlistair wanted him, and what would happen if he got him. The knowledge made his hands clammy with fear.

Aiming for the back of town, Tyler spurred the Appaloosa around a corner. If he could stay away from any roads, he knew he had a chance. Not many could follow him when he used his rabbit-hunting trails. He saw the cottonwoods at the edge of town in front of him and breathed deeply of the hot air. The Appaloosa, feeling his panic, raced faster.

A rider cut in behind him, a second from the side. Tyler knew he'd been caught, but he wasn't about to give in without a fight. His hands light on the reins, he leaned forward and urged more speed from the Appaloosa. Flying over the rough ground, the Appaloosa seemed to edge away from the pursuers. Then, all at once, the horse's pace changed and he began slowing down.

"No, no!" Tyler shouted, pushing the animal. But the leg was lame, and jerking to a ragged trot, the Appaloosa ground down eventually to a halt.

Guns pulled, the two men grinned. "Well, well! Looks like this one was easy pickings, huh, Jimmy?" one said. With knowing eyes, he leaned down to take the reins from Tyler's hands.

Gasping for breath, Tyler snatched away from the outlaw and flung himself to the ground. His knees almost buckled with the shock, but he split out at a run. He wasn't going to give in that easily.

With a cackle, Jimmy fired the .45. The bullet ripped into Tyler's side, spinning him like a top. The last thing he saw was the brown dirt.

"I didn't want him dead, you sorry piece of scum!" McAlistair backhanded Jimmy.

"But, boss, he's not dead! Just winged him, was all!" The gunhawk swiped at his bleeding nose, his temper barely in check.

McAlistair stared into his minion's eyes, the man's fear and anger feeding his ego like a shot of whisky. "He'd better not die, or you're a goner!" His voice was soft with anticipation.

Tyler groaned. The waves of pain washing over him pulled him out of the darkness. "Huh," he croaked, rolling over. *Bad move,* he thought with sudden clarity as something stabbed him in the side like a knife. As he focused on the faces surrounding him, it all came back: the run on the Appaloosa, the blast that had thrown him to the ground, and the nothingness that had followed.

His side was warm and sticky. But it was the face of the Scotsman that held his attention like a magnet.

"Well, laddie, I see you've decided to rejoin us." Squatting on the floor beside Tyler, McAlistair gave him a twisted smile. Tyler pushed at the dirt floor of the stable with both hands, trying to rise to his feet. McAlistair clamped his shoulder with an iron fist. "Stay put, boy, if you know what's good for you."

Tyler obeyed. "I'm not afraid of you!" His voice cracked. The *pistoleros* hooted.

McAlistair stood, hitching up his pants. "Well, you should be. Because if you don't tell me what I want to know, I'll kill you." He spoke with a singsong rhythm to his words, as if telling a fairy tale to a young child.

Tyler glanced around. Five men, guns slung low, their eyes long since dead, leered down at him like hungry wolves. A shapeless bundle in the corner by the front door caught his attention. He knew from the boots that it was Tomas, the Mexican.

"What do you want with me?" Tyler knew he might as well be already dead. The only thing that mattered was throwing the scent away from the marshal. It wasn't the first time Tyler had faced death. The cold stone in the pit of his stomach was gone, just as it had disappeared when his parents were killed, and when Quanta had come after him at Miss Hope's. Death was a fact that he could live with. He just wasn't going to let anyone else die for him, not Tomas, not anyone.

"Where's Moses, the marshal?" McAlistair's words could have cut rock. "Now, boy. Tell me, *now!*"

"Don't know. He's out there, though, and he'll get you!"

The *pistoleros* hooted as McAlistair slapped Tyler back to the floor.

"No games with me, you wet-nosed kid! Think

I won't kill you? Well, guess again." McAlistair gently placed the end of his .45 to Tyler's temple. Shutting his eyes, Tyler tried to recite the Lord's Prayer. His fingers were icy cold. McAlistair clicked back the action. "Where's the marshal? One more time, and you'd better answer, or it's the last chance you'll get to say words on this earth!"

"I swear, I don't know. He's coming into town, wanted me to warn Miss Wynoma so she could get outta the way!" Tyler's voice squeaked. "It's God's truth!"

McAlistair released the action, the trembling in the boy doing the convincing. "All right, so when's he coming in?"

"Don't know that, either. He just told me to get Miss Wynoma and get outta town. God's truth!" he repeated. Sensing his act was working, Tyler opened his eyes. McAlistair's gaze was on his henchmen.

"I want every man jack of you on the roof. Get the others in here, and be quick about it!"

His attention diverted, McAlistair turned from Tyler. He strode toward the shaft of light falling from the crack in the livery door, then paused. "Oh, and bring the boy. We may need him." Tyler's heart sank. Rough hands hauled him to his feet, and two men dragged him along behind McAlistair.

The hubbub in the street stopped as McAlistair halted in front of the livery. "Make sure you keep things as usual," he snarled at one of the *pistoleros.* "I don't want the marshal to guess we're laying a trap for him."

"Sure thing, Mr. McAlistair." Two others moved out, spitting commands to those on the street. Tyler watched as the others barked to their fellow bushwhackers and they disappeared into storefronts. Soon, rifles shone from second-story windows and rooftops. Tyler, hanging by his arms between the two men, counted every one.

"Take him to my office!" Dismissing Tyler, McAlistair turned his full attention to his strategy. "You there, Jimmy! Move to the right. I want that side covered!" Gesturing like a general planning a battle, McAlistair snapped orders.

Tyler was bound and thrown on the rough plank floor of the back room that served as McAlistair's office. Alone, he reviewed every gunman's position he'd seen, and he knew he had to work free. It was his only chance. Because if the marshal was killed, he was dead also. And so was Miss Wynoma. He began struggling with the ropes, his hands already raw and bleeding from the rough hemp of the knots.

It seemed like hours later, and he was still not free. The setting sun cast pale pinks and reds onto the floor as Tyler wearily laid his cheek to the rough planks beneath him. It was too late. All he wanted now was sleep.

Chapter Seventeen

PEDRO Sanchez's lathered horse stumbled to a halt at the Hamill place. "Wynoma!" the man croaked, his throat clogged with dust. "Wynoma, it's me, Sanchez!"

Wynoma flew onto the porch, Moses just behind her. "What is it, Pedro? What's happened?" She knew something was dreadfully wrong, and that had to mean Tyler.

"I went into town to get supplies yesterday, and I saw the whole thing. You gotta get outta here. He'll be coming after you when he's through with that marshal!" The man's gasps were as jagged as the horse's.

Moses stepped down, grabbing the farmer by the shoulders. "What happened? How does he know I'm here?"

"Got Tyler, that boy of Miss Hope's. I saw him dragged out of the livery, and next thing, I hear McAlistair shouting to his men to cover from the roofs, every corner of town. I put two and two together and lit out afore they could figure out I was there to begin with."

Wynoma fetched him a ladle of water. "What about Tyler, Pedro? Was he alive?"

"Yeah, McAlistair ordered them to take him somewhere. Looked like he'd been winged, but he was breathing."

Moses tied down his gun while striding for the barn. "Wynoma, you stay here. If I'm not back in two hours, you get going. Hear me?" Turning to her suddenly, he stopped in midmove. "And don't look back. It'll mean we're both dead, me and Tyler."

Wynoma watched him turn and walk away as though he wanted his feet to bruise the ground. She knew he was right.

Chloe clattered out of the barn, Moses already mounted. Pedro, his dark face tight with fatigue, watched him go.

"What now, Wynoma?"

"I darn sure don't aim to sit here and do nothing. It's time this ended, that we got rid of McAlistair. Are you with me, Pedro?" Wynoma ran for the house, her mind made up.

Following her, Pedro hung in the doorway. "You know that, Wynoma. But there's nothing we can do, nothing at all. McAlistair's got more men than dogs got fleas."

"But he won't be expecting the marshal to have any help, will he? Think you can get out to the Brown place, tell them to get everyone to town they can, bring their rifles? There's gotta be a way we can stop McAlistair."

"But—" Pedro started to protest.

Wynoma loaded the rifle on Hope's mantel, her fingers clicking in shells. Stopping for a second, she held his gaze. "I'm going to town, with or without anyone else. If you feel like coming along, fine. My mind's made up." The ferocity of her words humbled him.

"I'll get going, start with Emma and her man. What'll I tell them?"

"The truth. That we're going against McAlistair. That the marshal needs our help. That Tyler needs us."

Pedro watched her mount the mule, the rifle under her arm. He followed her out, his tired horse pushed once more to the limits. It was going to be a day when they all would find the extent of their own courage. Wynoma had more than enough for them all.

It was dark by the time Moses reached the outskirts of town. Settling into the stand of cottonwoods nearby, he dismounted and loosened Chloe's girth. Next he checked his weapons.

"Can't go barging in with guns blazing, can I, girl?" Chloe nudged him on the shoulder. "What do you think of a little disguise?" He almost laughed. "Kinda hard to disguise this black skin, huh?"

But he knew there had to be a back way. Somehow, he'd find Tyler and get him out first. He had to. Reviewing in his mind's eye the sheriff's office and its location in relation to McAlistair's hangout, he guessed they had Tyler in one of the two places. McAlistair would want someone to keep his eye on the boy at all times, which meant Moses would have to make sure the alarm didn't get sounded when he went in.

Drawing the knife from his boot, he tested it with his thumb. Replacing it, he dropped Chloe's reins. She'd stay where he left her, until hell froze over.

Setting out at a steady jog, he soon found himself nearing town, and pale pools of light shone from the windows into the street. Breathing hard, he flattened himself against a wall, then leaned around a corner to check it out.

The moon was full enough to cast a pure, white light on the town McAlistair had taken over and made into a den of iniquity. Moses' instincts told him there were more bodies around than there should have been, and they were doing their darnedest to stay hidden. A quick flash of a match from a rooftop caught his eye. *So,* he thought, *they're expecting a frontal assault.*

Creeping around the back, he waited with each few steps to hear any more movement. Nearing the back of the jail, he wished he'd brought Chloe so he could look into the window of the lone cell. Finally, gouging out a toehold in the wall, he got enough of a grip to raise himself to the barred window.

Empty. He cursed silently. That meant McAlistair had the boy with him, and he'd have to get to the other side of the street. Moving silently, he edged his way toward the livery stable, set at an angle to the main part of town. There'd be only about twenty-five feet of open road that he'd have to run. Hearing the snore of one of the sentries in the livery, he paused to make sure there was no one else. A murmur of voices reached him from his right.

Crouching behind a pile of manure and straw, Moses waited for them to pass.

"I'm getting tired of all this. He's not gonna come riding in here. No one's that much of a fool!"

"Quit your bellyaching, Sipes. Think I like this any more than you? Just shaddup and keep your eyes open!"

As soon as they circled the corner, Moses began his dodge across the roadway. Counting the facades, he guessed which one was McAlistair's lair. Hiding behind every available rain barrel, he worked his way up the street. A hum of voices rose from the saloon. Glasses tinkled, a hand slammed the bar, and silence reigned again.

Moses checked every window he could reach. A man like McAlistair would have no rear exit from his refuge, Moses figured. He'd be afraid of backshooters getting him from behind. Still, he found the right place, he thought, as he peeked around a sill to see a large oak desk and a wall cabinet filled with Winchesters. Only McAlistair would keep an arsenal in front of him.

He worried the window with his fingers, testing to see how much it would creak. There was a rattle of loose panes and a slight groan of old wood as he lifted the sash. The glass globe on the desk gave off an oily, dirty light. Still, he couldn't see anyone.

"Tyler?" He ventured a soft call to the boy. No response. He lifted himself over the sill with powerful shoulders, and landed like a cat inside. "Tyler?" The boy had to be there.

"Mmmpf." The strangled sound, with a thud against a wall from the next room, answered him. His knife drawn, Moses crouched. He had to get through the closed door, and there was no way of knowing what or who was there.

Nudging the door open, Moses crept through it. Tyler, bound and gagged, rolled on the floor in front of him, his eyes teary with joy.

Moses gestured for him to keep silent as he sliced through the hemp and removed the gag. Shaking his head in response to Tyler's unspoken questions, he rubbed the boy's wrists and ankles. Tyler grimaced with pain. Pointing to the blood caking Tyler's shirt at the ribs, Moses frowned a question about the wound. Tyler shrugged, signifying by his actions that it was nothing.

Moses seethed inside. Tyler looked so young and vulnerable, and yet a hundred years old at the same time. Helping him to his feet, Moses locked his arm about the boy's waist. Pointing to the opened window, he lifted Tyler along the floor. The return of circulation to Tyler's cramped limbs almost caused him to cry out.

Moses nodded in sympathy. He'd see that McAlistair paid for this, but first he had to get Tyler somewhere safe. Just as he was lifting Tyler through the window, the door to the street crashed open. Dropping Tyler, Moses drew and fired.

A blur of motion swept across the room, with Moses' shots spitting forth like letters on a telegraph key. One figure sprawled in the doorway, the others trampled over him.

"Tyler, run for it!" Moses found his voice as the lead flew around them. Tyler bolted through the window headfirst, fear making him forget his painful legs and arms.

"Don't kill him. McAlistair said he wants him for himself!" The command, barked in irritation, was lost in the fusillade of gunfire Moses showered upon the *pistoleros*. Backing through the window, Moses glanced down at the ground to make sure Tyler had cleared.

Gripping Tyler by the throat, McAlistair held the boy like a rag doll. "Drop the gun, Marshal, or he's dead."

Moses dropped it. Tyler sobbed.

Chapter Eighteen

WYNOMA walked the last bit into town, her breath coming in short gasps. She knew it was fear that was cutting her lung capacity, not the exertion. Even in the last heat of the night, her hands were clammy on the rifle, her dress clinging to her in huge cold patches. *Lord, Lord,* she prayed as she edged in the back way, *let me know what's right to do, and I'll do it.*

She had no idea where to start. For all she knew, Moses had found Tyler and hidden him somewhere while biding his time to go in after McAlistair. The full moon shed a false picture of brightness on the small buildings of the town, and Wynoma knew she'd have to be careful. It would be too easy to spot her light-colored dress.

"Vera?" Slipping inside the small house where Vera lived with her mother, Wynoma called out softly. "Vera, it's Wynoma. You awake?"

A light appeared from the room cordoned off from the rest of the shack by a calico curtain. Stepping forward quickly, Wynoma gestured for Vera to blow out the lamp.

"Don't wake your mother, but I need your help."

Vera pulled on a robe as she left her mother sleeping in the same bed. "Land's sakes, Miss Wynoma, you're durned and determined to get yourself killed, I just know it!"

Pulling Vera into the other room, Wynoma checked the street from the small window. "Hope not. You know where McAlistair is? The marshal came in after Tyler, and—"

She could tell from the expression on Vera's face that it was bad.

Vera shook her head. "McAlistair was waiting, found Tyler at the livery, got the marshal next. There's nothing you can do, Miss Wynoma, 'cept stay out of it, or you're dead for sure."

Pulling the rifle out from its wrapping in her apron, Wynoma opened the door.

"Where are they, Tyler and the marshal?"

"Don't know for sure. Saw them dragged down the street to the livery. They done killed the old Mexican who took care of cleaning the place. Guess they're still alive, though, 'cause I ain't heard any gunshots. Not recently, that is."

"You stay here, keep your eyes open. Pedro Sanchez's gone to find help. I 'spect he'll be here close to sun-up. You tell him what you've told me, and let him know I'm waiting near the livery for him."

Vera's hands kneaded her robe. "What if he don't come? Then what?"

Wynoma shrugged. "Restaurant's yours, if you want it. But if I was you, I'd get outta McAlistair and stay gone. Long as McAlistair's around, there's no way you or anyone else is gonna be free."

Sliding into the night, Wynoma worked her way softly around the back of town to the livery. There was no way she could do it alone, but she'd make sure McAlistair didn't live, even if she had to backshoot him. *God, forgive me,* she pleaded silently, staring at the butternut-yellow pool of light coming from the livery. *I'm about to commit murder, and break one of your commandments. But I'll do it,* she pledged as she hid behind the manure pile.

Spreading some of the dirty straw and muck around her, she tried to keep from gagging at the strong, ammonialike smell. But McAlistair's men, if they were watching, wouldn't be paying attention to the manure. Listening intently, she could hear the wildness of voices inside, none of them belonging to Moses or Tyler, she was sure. Edging closer to the stable, she crept farther into the muck.

Her hands felt flesh, cold and stiff. Pushing her hand against her mouth, she gagged a cry. *Dear Heavenly Father, no, no!* Pleading with all her heart, she dug into the straw, careless of the noise she made. *It couldn't be, it won't be,* she bargained with God, *if You'll let him live, I'll do anything, anything.* Reaching the dead man's head, she laid down the rifle to pull him into the moonlight. A burst of laughter split the night from the livery.

Tracing the features with her fingers, Wynoma knew it wasn't Moses. The old Mexican's eyes reflected the moonbeams, and Wynoma stroked the lids shut with her palms. Cradling him in her arms, she gave a guilty prayer of thanks that it wasn't the marshal.

The light of a cigarette burst the night close to her, and she froze in the act of re-covering the Mexican with the straw. "When we gonna get our fun, I wonder?" The cigarette bounced in the speaker's lips.

"No telling. McAlistair'll have his first. Probably won't give us much leavin's. Don't know why we're out here—everyone knows the marshal was alone."

"Yeah, well, you be the one to tell the boss we're tired of guard duty out here. I'll wait for you to get your tail back here."

The man with the cigarette spit it out. "The devil you will. I ain't that dumb."

Their voices receded around the corner. Calculating the distance to the side of the barn, Wynoma hiked up her skirts and ran for it. Stifling her gasps, she found a crack in the weathered boards and watched.

McAlistair sat on an old Army chair as though it were a throne, his scepter a pistol. Drunken men surrounded him like knights, passing a bottle of rotgut from man to man as they took turns.

"Think he needs stretching a little tighter, boss? If you want this hide cured good, we gotta stretch it real tight!" One of the *pistoleros* tightened the knot around Moses' wrist. Wynoma felt her stomach heave at the sight of the marshal, spread-eagled between stalls, his hands and legs tied with heavy rope.

His face was gray and shiny with sweat, but his eyes never left McAlistair's face. She could see the knotted muscles and veins in his neck and down his front where the shirt had been torn by a whip. She forced herself to shut her eyes, to try to wipe out the image, and knew it was something she'd never forget. *Stop it!* she told herself. *Stop this shaking, or you won't be able to help.*

She knew the only way she could help. McAlistair wanted torture, not death. Death would rob him of all his pleasure, and she was the only one who could do that. Desperately, she made herself look again, trying to figure out how she could get off a shot that would kill McAlistair before they got her. The crack in the boards wasn't wide enough, and her aim was shaky at its best. She'd have to get closer, and that meant going in.

Tyler. She'd almost forgotten him in the horror of seeing Moses. Inching her way down the crack in the board, she tried to see the boy. A small, shapeless bundle in a corner of the light from the lamp caught her attention. Focusing on it, she saw Tyler's boots. He wasn't moving.

Flicking the bullwhip with a casual wrist, McAlistair sent another streak of red across Moses' shirt.

"No, no!" Tyler screamed. "You can't do this! You're a bunch of—" A boot thudded into his side, and Tyler whimpered.

It came to her. The straw dust swirled as Tyler rolled, away from the hurricane lantern hanging on a nail. Working the barrel of the rifle through the crack, she aimed. If she missed, there wasn't going to be a second chance.

She heard the grumbles of the guards as they rounded the corner. Letting out her breath, she squeezed the trigger. The report of the rifle rang out like a crack of thunder as the bullet shattered the lantern.

Spreading shards of glass and oil, the old lantern toppled into the straw. Instantly, tendrils of flames crept across the livery floor, following the path of the oil. Frozen, the gunhawks stared at the small fire, growing bigger by the instant, until it dawned upon them that the combustion hadn't been a spontaneous one.

"Where'd that come from?" McAlistair roared, toppling the chair over as he spun around to search. "Get him, you lazy louts!" His pistol twirled with him, pointing first at one, then another of his henchmen.

Realizing that McAlistair thought there was

a traitor in his midst, Wynoma flattened against the wall of the stable, knowing she'd be seen in the next moment. But the guards, hearing McAlistair's command from inside, raced for the door of the livery. Plastering her eye to the crack once more, she saw the smoke begin. It might give her the cover she needed.

Shouts crescendoed as the gunhawks realized that the fire was spreading quickly. "Get water!" McAlistair held his gun on his own men as he snapped the command. Watching him like rattlers about to strike, the gunhawks edged toward the livery door in the sudden darkness, their hands close to their holsters.

"Sure, boss, just a minute. . . ." One of them stepped out of the retreating line and made a move toward the Scotsman.

"So it's you!" McAlistair fired, sending the surprised *pistolero* sprawling.

"Let's get outta here!" The shout rose above the increasing crackle of the flames. As one body, the *pistoleros* stampeded for the street. "Let him burn—serve him right!"

Wynoma crouched behind the doors as they were flung open, watching the retreat of McAlistair's dogs and wanting desperately to shoot every one of them in the back for what they'd done to Moses. But there wasn't enough time, and she knew her revenge would have to wait. Stepping into the thick smoke of the livery, she heard the horses screaming for the first time.

On the Terror Trail   181

Squatting beside Tyler, she put her hand on his opened mouth. He nodded. She stood, barely able to make out McAlistair, his gun in Moses' mouth, his face twisted with insanity as he spewed forth obscenities at the marshal.

"Here, McAlistair." She spoke calmly, the rifle at her shoulder.

Firing as the Scotsman, slack-jawed, spun to stare at her, she caught him square in the middle. Arms flung wide, McAlistair recoiled with the shot and landed at Moses' feet.

For the first time, she let herself look Moses in the eyes. "Come on, Marshal. Let's get outta here."

Sawing at the knots with her fingers, she felt frantic. "Not much time." Finally, she bit at the hemp, chewing through the cords that bound Moses.

In silence, she pulled him free, and helped him stumble to where Tyler was still tied. Letting the marshal's arm fall from her shoulder, she searched for a knife to cut the boy's bonds.

"No time for that." Moses coughed. With his torn and bleeding palms, he lifted Tyler in his arms and stumbled for the door. With a swoosh, the stored bales of hay and straw ignited, the force of the blast of hot air tossing them to the ground like rag dolls.

Dawn was streaking the sky with bits of red as they sprawled outside, gasping for untainted air, heaving chests trying to clear their lungs.

Dragging herself to her knees, Wynoma crawled to Tyler to try his knots again. Looking up, she expected to see the *pistoleros* ringing them like wolves, but at this point, she didn't really care. They'd made it this far, they'd survive.

Pedro Sanchez and the other farmers held the gunhawks in their sights. "You okay, Wynoma? What about the boy, the marshal?"

Wynoma's tears streaked her face as she smiled. "We're fine, Pedro. Just fine."

Moses stood slowly and nodded in return. His eyes held hers like magnets as he silently thanked her for more than his life.

Chapter Nineteen

Moses wouldn't let Tyler go with him to Fort Smith when they took in the *pistoleros*. Tyler had watched the marshal ride out, his chest bandaged, the other farmers riding with him, and Wynoma had held him close. She knew the boy's latent fear that the marshal wouldn't come back this time. They waited the weeks together, mostly in silence. Now and then, Tyler would pull the volume of Keats from its chamois cover and read a few lines out loud to her, stumbling over words as he did so. Often, she traced the lines in her palm, realizing that the soothsayer had seen that she'd kill a man written in the swirls in her skin.

She had just finished the dishes when Tyler shouted from the front porch, "He's coming! He's coming!" It had been many long weeks for her too, and she dropped the cup back into the soapy water as she raced to smooth her hair and untie her apron.

Moses looked firmer in the saddle, as though the act of bringing McAlistair's men to justice had healed many wounds. Waving, she wondered what he planned to do next. Tyler tore into the street, racing to hang onto Moses' stirrup. Reaching down, the marshal heaved the gangly boy up behind him onto the cantle. Chloe did a hippity-hop, and started to lope.

Laughing, Moses dropped Tyler at Wynoma's feet. "Brought you something."

She smiled at the mischief in his eyes. "Don't need another crazy boy like this one, thank you much," she said, and Tyler glared.

"Nothing quite that drastic. But almost." Pointing at his weathered hide vest, he waited for her to notice the unfaded spot where the badge had hung for so long.

She'd be gol-durned if she'd cry. Biting her lip, she nodded. "Ever tried farming?"

"Nope. But I figure there's plenty you know about it. Make you a bargain: I'll teach you reading and writing, you teach me good farming." Swinging down from the saddle, he looked her square in the eyes, his shoulders tense.

"Do my best. I'll make you a good wife, Leland Moses." Reaching for his hand, she pulled him to her.

"I know you will, Wynoma Webster." Every inch of his face was a smile.

"Tyler, think you can stand another piece of pie? You and me and the marshal, we better get started planning how we can make Miss Hope's place ours. Way I see it, Tyler's her next of kin, leastwise that's the way most folks see it, and. . . ."

Chattering excitedly, she led the way into the restaurant, one of Moses' hands in hers, Tyler hanging on the other.

Fort Loudoun Regional Library

Dunham   FL 254122
On the Terror Trail
$13.95

CAT CARDS

DATE DUE

Dunham   FL 254122
On the Terror Trail
$13.95

CAT CARDS

DATE	ISSUED TO
	Gladys Dapin
6/1/90	Herbert Sims
6/2/20	

FORT LOUDOUN REGIONAL LIBRARY
718 GEORGE ST., NW
ATHENS, TN 37303

On the Terror Trail
F Dun   46958

Dunham, Tracy
Rockwood Public Library